"I'll make a trade, El. I'll give you the microphone back if you give me what I want," Douglas told her.

She shivered. "What would you be wanting?"

He met her eyes with a gaze that had suddenly become intense. "Five minutes of you. Just standing here and not making any n̶____"

Elgiva understood pe____ ____ and her knees grew weak. "I'll ju____

"No, you wo____ ____ terrible to you. I thi____ ____ ot want to leave w____

"No. E____ ____ monster."

"How r____ ____oned her close to the bars of his____ ____denly his face was only a hand's widt____ ____ers. The heat and scent of his body radiated over her; his breath brushed across her cheeks.

"Set?" he asked softly. She could barely think, much less speak. She nodded. "Go."

His hand slipped between the bars and slid up under her loose hair. "Tilt your head back a little," he ordered softly, and when she did, he kissed her lips until she was helpless with desire. He was dissolving her reason and resistance, giving her what she'd always longed for and never known. She couldn't stop kissing him—until his mouth moved from hers and he spoke hoarsely. "How many nightgowns do you have?"

"Two," she murmured, dazed with sensation.

"Good. I don't want you to do without later." With only that warning he ripped her gown down the center, and Elgiva cried out in shock and even wilder excitement. . . .

WHAT ARE *LOVESWEPT* ROMANCES?

They are stories of true romance and touching emotion. We believe those two very important ingredients are constants in our highly sensual and very believable stories in the *LOVESWEPT* line. Our goal is to give you, the reader, stories of consistently high quality that may sometimes make you laugh, sometimes make you cry, but are always fresh and creative and contain many delightful surprises within their pages.

Most romance fans read an enormous number of books. Those they truly love, they keep. Others may be traded with friends and soon forgotten. We hope that each *LOVESWEPT* romance will be a treasure—a "keeper." We will always try to publish

LOVE STORIES YOU'LL NEVER FORGET
BY AUTHORS YOU'LL ALWAYS REMEMBER

The Editors

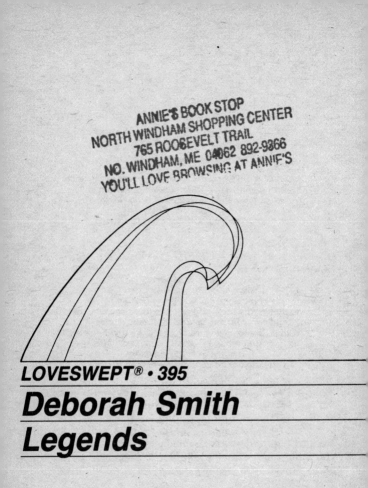

LOVESWEPT® • 395

Deborah Smith
Legends

BANTAM BOOKS
NEW YORK • TORONTO • LONDON • SYDNEY • AUCKLAND

LEGENDS

A Bantam Book / April 1990

LOVESWEPT® and the wave device are registered
trademarks of Bantam Books, a division of
Bantam Doubleday Dell Publishing Group, Inc.
Registered in U.S. Patent
and Trademark Office and elsewhere.

If you would be interested in receiving protective vinyl
covers for your Loveswept books, please write to this address
for information:

Loveswept
Bantam Books
P.O. Box 985
Hicksville, NY 11802

ISBN 0-553-44026-8

Published simultaneously in the United States and Canada

Bantam Books are published by Bantam Books, a division
of Bantam Doubleday Dell Publishing Group, Inc. Its trademark, consisting of the words "Bantam Books" and the
portrayal of a rooster, is Registered in U.S. Patent and
Trademark Office and in other countries. Marca Registrada.
Bantam Books, 666 Fifth Avenue, New York, New York 10103.

PRINTED IN THE UNITED STATES OF AMERICA

OPM   0 9 8 7 6 5 4 3 2 1

One

Everything was right with Douglas Kincaid's world. Behind him, a wall of magnificent windows show-cased the glitter of Manhattan at night. He owned those windows sixty stories up with their awe-inspiring view. He also owned the fifty-nine stories below his Gucci-loafered feet. In fact he owned the entire skyscraper, which was named, with Douglas Kincaid's usual humility, Kincaid Place.

He owned many other buildings, companies, and homes all over the world. He loved each one. Whether he sold one or traded one or bought many at a time, he always, *always*, put his name on a building or an enterprise he owned. Even the champion golden retriever who lay at his feet was named Kincaid's Mighty Majestic. But because Douglas Kincaid didn't take himself as seriously as the public and the media suspected, he privately called his dog Sam.

"Fetch, Sam. Get the Casner's," he said now, and Sam trotted to a gilt-and-lacquer bar in one corner of the huge room, where he rose on his hind legs and took a bottle of premium Scotch whisky in his powerful jaws.

Sam returned to his master's side and woofed in satisfaction when Douglas caressed his head. After splashing Scotch into a crystal tumbler, Douglas set the bottle on a glistening Art Deco side table, sipped his drink, and sighed with contentment.

Outside his darkly elegant office snow drifted over the city. Inside an exquisite music system whispered a seductive jazz selection. The atmosphere was perfect for his reflective mood. The night, New Year's Eve, was perfect for beginning a new venture. He finished his drink, rubbed his hands together in anticipation, and grinned.

Douglas Kincaid was ready to put his name on a wife.

He leaned back in an opulent wing-backed chair, gave a droll salute to the party going on beyond a one-way wirror, then pressed the button on a speakerphone. "All right, Gert, let's go through the list."

An exasperated sigh preceded his assistant's French-accented voice. "They're all so unworthy, Monsieur K!"

He chuckled. "I have to start somewhere. Blondes are just round one. Go ahead, Gert."

"Always the blondes, yes. There are five of them. If you will look to the right of the Picasso near the staircase, you'll see the Duchess of Atworth. She's speaking with Monsieur and Madame Trump."

Douglas studied the packed ballroom framed by the one-way mirror in his hideaway. Finally he spotted the Duchess, engaged in animated conversation with his friends Donald and Ivana. "Not bad," he told Gert. "But too young."

"The older ones are more demanding."

"I like a challenge. Next?"

"The singer Platinum. You recall she sent you that autographed bit of lingerie? She is seated at the grand piano with the maestro."

"Hmmm. She seems to be tickling him while he tickles the ivories. I need a woman with more discretion—and much better taste in clothes. Black leather and sequins aren't the style in evening gowns this season, are they?"

"Only in Hollywood, Monsieur."

"Next."

"Beside the waterfall, flicking her cigarette ashes into Monsieur's priceless crystal vase, is the state supreme court judge who fixed Monsieur's parking ticket."

He smiled. "I'm likely to marry her just to taste nicotine again. I can't risk that kind of temptation. Next?"

"A moment, Monsieur K. I'm searching."

While he waited, Douglas let his gaze drift over the crowd and impatiently tapped a finger on the arm of his chair. Suddenly his field of vision was filled completely with shimmering green silk wrapped around a tall and very voluptuous female body.

Sam woofed softly.

"I agree," Douglas told him.

His one-way mirror had been overwhelmed by glorious feminine curves swathed in a clinging, floor-length gown. Their owner was so tall and so close that the mirror could only capture her from the neck down. Except for the glass wall between them, Douglas could have reached out his hand and touched her, something he found himself very interested in doing.

She bent over and gazed at herself in the mirror, unknowingly presenting him with an intimate close-up of a mature, beautiful face plus a mane of elegantly shaggy blond hair that looked as if a man's hands had just ruffled it.

Staring straight at him were large eyes the amber color of his Scotch. She pursed a regal, almost solemn mouth and checked its tinted edges with the tip of a glossy nail. Wrinkling a proudly sculptured nose, she blew a kiss at herself, though it could have been aimed at Douglas. Leaning even closer to the mirror, she adjusted her low-slung bodice. Douglas suddenly found himself admiring a stunning pair of barely covered breasts.

Gert's exasperated sputtering came over the speakerphone. "*Mon Dieu*! She's an exhibitionist! She's brought her melons to market and put them on display!"

Douglas fell back in his chair and roared with laughter, but he couldn't take his eyes off the big, beautiful woman who had usurped his whole mirror. Elemental sensations slipped through his blood, and his laughter faded as breath deserted him. "Who is she?" he demanded quickly, his eyes never leaving her.

"Uhmmm, let's see . . . let's see . . ." He could hear Gert shuffling papers in her office. She yelped softly. "I have no photograph of this one, no statistics, nothing. She isn't on my list! How could this have happened? She's a gate-crasher! But how—oh, those fools in security! I'll have their heads for this. This has never happened before. Are they all asleep?"

"Stunned, not asleep, I imagine." Douglas continued to gaze admiringly at the woman, who was now running the tip of her tongue across a smudge of color on her lower lip. Douglas leaned forward and placed large, blunt fingers against the glass directly across from her provocatively moving tongue. Raw desire whipped through him so swiftly that he shivered.

Frowning at her power, he withdrew his hand. She must be smart, if she could get past one of the best security teams money could hire. All she had probably had to do was turn those odd, golden eyes on them, and they had been hypnotized. Much as he was now.

She was dressed to provoke male fantasies, but there was nothing sleazy about her. There was, instead, something mysterious.

Around her neck she wore a simple gold chain. Hanging from it was a fascinating pendant with an aged, antique look about it. Stamped into the gold were a pair of rams locked in combat. Above them and to their left stood a fierce-looking griffin. He was separated from the embattled rams by a sword, but also he seemed to be distant from them in attitude, watching them with an air of superiority.

"Do you wish for me to call security?" Gert asked. "Monsieur? Are you there?"

Douglas abruptly realized how mesmerized he was by the combination of the blonde's eyes and the pendant. He rubbed his forehead. "Don't report this, Gert. Just go out and talk to her. Tell her I'd like to invite her to my office for a glass of champagne."

"As you wish, Monsieur K."

Douglas flicked a switch on the phone console, and the mirror went dark. He shut his eyes and relished the moment when he'd meet his incredible gate-crasher in person. A minute later the phone beeped.

"Monsieur? She is eager for an introduction." Gert's voice held a tone of polite disgust. "But she asks to visit Kincaid Park. Such arrogance!"

Douglas laughed again. The blonde had studied him. She knew about his private forest atop the building. He liked her attention to detail—especially since it concerned him—and he liked her assertive attitude. "All right. I'll grab a coat and go up right now. Tell her it'll be cold. Provide a coat if she doesn't have something warm enough."

"Yes. She appears to be unaccustomed to covering herself."

Douglas rose from his chair and gestured for Sam to follow. Where he went in the world, Sam went also, whether to a business meeting, a charity ball, a boxing match, or to meet a beautiful woman.

When Douglas stepped out of the elevator into the man-made forest atop his penthouse, he found the blonde waiting. She wore an emerald-green cape that matched her dress. It swirled around her from shoulders to feet. Lamps hidden in the shrubbery cast shadows on her that lent her an even greater air of mystery. Her face was teasingly obscured by the cape's hood, but he couldn't miss her slow, deliberate smile, filled with invitation.

Douglas felt his pulse throb in the most masculine places, but also acknowledged an unusual feeling of fascination. The wind whipped the cape, molding it to her statuesque body. Douglas raised the cashmere collar of his overcoat and gallantly swept a hand toward a path in the forest. "Please. It's less windy among the trees."

She nodded but didn't say a word. Growing more intrigued by the second, Douglas watched her glide into the thick fir woods as if she were a beautiful phantom disappearing into a land of giant Christmas trees. Sam galloped after her, as if compelled. Douglas followed with long, hurried strides, feeling a little ridiculous for being so easily led, but supremely confident that he'd have the upper hand soon.

She stopped and turned to face him. He halted also, and they gazed at each other in the shadows, no more than five feet apart. Snowflakes floated down around them. "Well, what do you think of New Year's Eve at Kincaid Park?" he asked. "Not bad for a kid who started out selling cheap soap on street corners, hmmm? Impressive, isn't it?"

He swung about slowly, his arms out, asking her to admire his hard-won paradise and comment appropriately. The second that he turned his back, he heard a soft popping sound. Something slapped him on the left side of the rump. Even through his thick overcoat, his tuxedo, and his custom-made underwear, he felt a sharp sting.

Douglas whirled around. Lethargy washed over him. He took a groggy step and swayed in place. She held a small pistol in one hand. She wasn't smiling anymore. Woozy, he craned his head and looked at his wounded hip. He fumbled with the long dart that protruded from his coat, and it fell to the soft pineneedle cushion of the forest floor.

He was not an easy man to conquer, and for a second fury nearly overcame narcotic bliss. After cursing viciously, he told her, "You'll never get it—whatever it is you want. My people have orders not to pay any ransoms."

She laughed. *Laughed.* Then she crossed her arms and watched him with an expression of undisguised victory on her face. Sam stepped forward and studied her closely, worried but curious. Sam had class; Sam wouldn't attack a woman. This one seemed to know that, because she clucked to him calmly, and he wagged his tail.

Douglas groaned with frustration as his bones seemed to melt. He sank to the ground, fury giving way to overpowering sleepiness. Rolling onto his back, he yawned helplessly. "Dammit. Dammit."

Dimly he was aware of the woman speaking to someone—not him, apparently, because her voice was too low. Sam came to him and lay down, oddly reassured, it seemed. He put his head on Douglas's shoulder. Then the woman walked over and knelt beside him, a radio in her hands, and he heard a metallic sliding sound as she collapsed the antenna.

"You can't get away with . . . whatever," Douglas protested, every word weighing heavy on his tongue.

The woman leaned over him, and he squinted up into her whisky eyes. Iced whisky, now. "You won't be telling me what I can and cannot do," she said. The Scottish burr in her voice was a shock. She chucked him under the chin.

"You're an *arrrogant* devil, Douglas Kincaid, and no credit to your Scot heritage. Now go to sleep. I don't mean any harm to you." She raised her head, tossed the cape back, and jerked off the blond wig. Chestnut-colored hair, glinting in the forest lamps, wound around the crown of her head in flat braids. She studied the snowy night sky.

Douglas groaned with frustration when he heard the whir of a helicopter. He tried to protest one more time, but now his mouth refused to work.

When she met his eyes again, he glared sleepily at her. The grim set of her mouth widened into a sardonic smile. "You've naught to frown over, my fine, handsome, worthless Mr. Kincaid. You're about to learn a lesson in humility, that's all."

The hell I will, he thought, and feel asleep.

Elgiva MacRoth didn't relax until she and her companions were on their ramshackle little airplane headed north over Canada. Getting Douglas Kincaid out of the city had been a terrifying experience, considering that the helicopter had nearly fallen apart.

Her cousin Andrew had warned, with great foresight, that the machine appeared to be in dubious condition and would probably be hard to maneuver. But they had had no choice. Happy to acquire a helicopter at all, they had gotten one only by bribing its drunken owner at a tiny, rural airfield in upstate New York.

Even now, far away from the dreadful helicopter, Elgiva didn't feel safe. Their cargo plane was protesting every minute of the journey back to Scotland. It was too old to be hopping all over the northern hemisphere in search of the shortest distance across the Atlantic. Each time Andrew landed it for refueling, the cabin walls rattled and the floor shook.

Considering their third-rate getaway vehicles and their absolute lack of criminal expertise, it was a wonder they'd managed to kidnap Douglas Kincaid at all. The fates were obviously on their side, she thought.

Using the wall struts to keep her balance, Elgiva staggered to the back. Douglas Kincaid's wonderful dog trailed her like an old friend. She went behind a curtain and changed the embarrassing green dress for tan corduroy trousers and a brightly colored sweater she had knitted herself. She slipped her feet into comfortable leather hiking shoes. The trappings of home began to soothe her nerves as she returned to her captive.

It was time to become more familiar with the man who was going to change—a less dedicated person might say *ruin*—her life. She took a chair beside a specially installed bed. "Aye, we're anxious for you to ride safely," she muttered to Kincaid. "You devil."

As she looked at his face, still set in lines of strength even while he slept, her heart rose in her throat. The next few weeks would go so much easier if he had been born ugly and dull. Elgiva never tried to rationalize her emotions; she might attack them with rigid discipline until they were subdued, but she never lied to herself about them.

So now she admitted that Douglas Kincaid was attractive, at least on a physical level. That didn't make her despise him any less, but she knew she'd have to deal with him as a provocative man as well as a prisoner, so she began preparing herself to do it.

Brusquely she unsnapped the belts that passed across his chest and thighs. "Your legs are too long and skinny for such a puffed-out rooster's chest," she taunted, as she unbuttoned his overcoat and flipped it back on both sides.

"And you've got big, mean hands like a gorilla's. Oh, I know all about you, Douglas. You were a boxer in your young years. Hmmmph! Someone pounded that nose a time or two, from the looks of it. What a crooked, nasty thing it is. Suits you—suits that thick, *belligerrrant* chin. I'll bet that some of your flashy white teeth are false, and the rest are capped."

She pushed one of his eyelids open. "Brown. Plain old brown, like the moors when all the heather has died for the winter." Her hand trembled. *Be honest,* she silently told herself. *They're like the dark, pretty eyes of a Terkleshire wolf.*

Elgiva made a soft sound of disgust and drew her hand away. "And such eyelashes! Only girls should have lashes so long and thick! You're not a real man, Douglas Kincaid." She glanced at the front of his tailored trousers. "You probably stuff a sock into your panties to give that grand show."

She stared for a moment, mesmerized, then angrily drew her attention to his head. She ruffled his hair with a rough hand. "Faith! Look at this black, wavy mess! Tamed with sprays and mousses, I'll warrant."

When she sank her fingers into his hair to inspect its coarse luxury further, a low, rich sound of pleasure rumbled from his throat. Elgiva jerked her hand away and watched him keenly. What appetites the man must have to sigh like that in his condition!

"If you come to, Douglas, you'll get popped with another round of sleepy-bye medicine." Just in case, she reached into her trouser pocket and rested her fingertips on the capped syringe there. Dr. Graham, the village physician, had provided an ample supply.

But after a moment it was obvious that Kincaid was still soundly drugged. A little dismayed by the fear he had provoked, she grabbed his head between her hands and glared down at him. "Where'd you get that starburst scar on your cheekbone, you mangy bull? I'll bet one of your ladyfriends whacked you with her diamond ring."

The skin of his cheeks was beginning to show a faint hint of black shadow. "You're just a furry savage," she observed primly. "For all your high-muckety-muck clothes and jewels, your clansmen were naught but hellions."

She ran her fingers down the front of his beautiful white shirt, trying to ignore the warmth and hardness of the chest underneath. "What ridiculous finery!" Set among crisp little pleats on his shirt front were onyx buttons rimmed in gold. A large diamond glittered in the center of each one.

Though she had studied him and his life-style, she was awed. Here was the embodiment of a fortune she could barely imagine, and while everything she cherished had taught her to reject such frippery, his use of it fascinated her. Combined with his brutally handsome face and body, the effect was potent. She molded her hand to his chest and slowly stroked the center, intrigued and a little breathless.

"Ellie! What're you doin' with him, lass?"

Her brother's incredulous voice made her whirl around in the chair. Rob had come back from the cockpit, but she hadn't even noticed. His eyes glittered with surprise and dismay.

Elgiva hadn't blushed in years; now she felt her face burning. Damn Douglas Kincaid! "I was just checking him over! Don't be sneaking up on me like that!" She whipped around and jammed a hand into one of Kincaid's trouser pockets. "I can't sit and stare at the beast, you know. I have to make sure that he has no weapons."

"His only weapon is between the covers of his bankbook," Rob replied grimly. "And inside that surpassin' devious mind of his."

And in other places that only a woman would think about, Elgiva added silently. Busying herself, she withdrew a set of keys from Kincaid's pockets. She muttered darkly, and Rob stepped closer to look over her shoulder. "Have you ever seen the like?" she asked. "Gold car keys with jewels set in them. And the names of the cars engraved. Porsche, Lamborghini, Jaguar, Rolls Royce, Lotus. How many automobiles can one man use? What're these? I don't recognize them."

"His classics. His 1936 Cord and 1938 Studebaker. Don't you remember from the magazine articles? The man is naught but a gangster. He loves all those American criminal styles from the thirties."

She tossed the keys onto a nearby seat. "That's his idea of history, I suppose. No wonder he didn't bother to find out about his true heritage. He'll be forced to, now."

"Aye." Rob's chestnut hair gleamed in the cabin lights as he bent forward to study the drugged billionaire. Her brother, his love for outlandish plaids subdued by caution, looked dashing in solid black trousers and a turtle-necked sweater.

She put a hand on Rob's broad shoulder. "You and Duncan should be putting on your ski masks, just in case Kincaid wakes for a moment. We should go to the cockpit and tell Andrew and Mrs. M to do the same."

Rob gave their sleeping prisoner one last frown. "You're right, Ellie. Let's not take any chances."

From the cabin came a sour-faced little man. Form-fitting black trousers and a turtle-neck red sweater were less kind to him than to Rob. "I'd like to make certain that the bastard doesn't see us," Duncan MacRoth sneered. He lumbered to Kincaid's side and jerked the man's head back roughly. "We ought to blindfold him so tight that his eyes burn for a week. A man like this won't cooperate unless you hurt him."

Duncan's ugly treatment of their prisoner infuriated Elgiva. Ordinarily the mayor of their village was merely pompous and overbearing. But he was afraid of Douglas Kincaid's power, as was everyone in Druradeen, and his fear made him cruel.

Elgiva bit her tongue and watched anxiously. From the corner of her eye she saw Rob stiffening with anger. Kincaid's dog shoved himself against Duncan's legs and snarled.

"Aye," Duncan continued grimly, and jerked Kincaid's head back a little farther. "We should bring him to Scotland wearing a few good bruises." He curled one hand up and started to slap him.

"No!" Elgiva and Rob said at the same time. Elgiva cupped her hands over Kincaid's face. "He's helpless, Duncan. He's my charge. And I say you won't hit him."

Kincaid's dog was now growling with a deep, wild tone. From the door to the cockpit came a crackling little voice. "Son? Duncan? We canna whack the poor helpless American unless he's awake. Now calm yourself."

Duncan stepped back, his eyes glazed with restrained anger. "I was just having a wee bit of fun with him, Mother." Elgiva shot an amused, grateful look at the elderly sprite in a black woolen dress.

Mirah MacRoth was Elgiva's second cousin four times removed, or some such thing—the clan genealogy was very complicated. Elgiva was glad to be related to Mrs. M, but sorry to be related to Mrs. M's son, Duncan, even if he was the best mayor the village had ever had.

"I can't wait to get this work done!" Duncan grumbled. "See that you don't muck it up, Elgiva!"

"Watch how you speak to my sister," Rob warned.

"Come, Duncan, and stop your naughtiness," Mrs. M ordered. Duncan would always be ten years old to her. She had been Druadeen's schoolmistress since 1949, and *every* adult in the village was still ten years old in spirit, as far as she was concerned.

Duncan stomped into the cockpit to sit with her and Andrew. After he slammed the door, Elgiva tilted Kincaid's head to a comfortable position and resisted an urge to smooth the hair Duncan had mussed. She stood quickly. "Best go and get your mask, Robbie. Duncan will pounce on the least excuse to complain."

Rob gripped Elgiva's arm and gazed hard into her eyes. "It's not too late for you to put on a mask too. We could change the plans."

She shook her head. "I suspect that Kincaid looked me over *verrry* well when I preened in front of his silly little one-way mirror. I don't think he's the kind of man who'd forget the details of his kidnapper's face." She hugged her brother and swallowed hard to keep the tears out of her voice. "It has to be this way, Robbie. If we get what we want, I won't be sorry. Sssh, now, you big-hearted brute."

She stood back and shook him lightly by the shoulders, as if he were still smaller than she. His handsome, angular features tightened with sorrow, and Elgiva tried to distract him. "Robbie, I think Mr. Kincaid's got you beat. He must be a good centimeter taller."

"Och! No!" Rob's eyes glittered with dismay, as she'd expected. "The thieving bastard's naught but a midget next to myself!"

"We'll bring him down a notch or two. Don't fret." Douglas Kincaid's dog licked her hand anxiously.

"Sssh, now, he'll be fine," she said soothingly, stroking the dog's broad, golden head. "It's me you should be worrying over, lad. I won't get out of this as well off as you and your grand friend here."

Rob touched her arm. "Go up and sit with the others, Ellie. I'm going to change his clothes."

"No. I'll help." At Rob's grim silence she glanced up. "Brother of mine, I was married for twelve years, you know. A man's body is nothing new to me. And if I'm going to be alone with this one for a whole month, I'll probably see more of him than I ever wanted."

He cursed softly. "I must have been crazy when we decided this plan. A true man wouldn't let his sister—"

"A true man knows when his sister is the best choice for a job. Now stop worrying!"

"If anything goes awry—"

"I'll have done what my heart and soul told me to do. Now come. Let's get this great, vain beast into some practical clothes."

Together they began undressing Douglas Kincaid. By the time they finished Elgiva was quivering inside from touching him, and she knew for certain that living alone with him for the next month would be more dangerous than she'd ever imagined.

Two

Douglas opened his eyes to a whitewashed wooden ceiling crisscrossed with rough beams. A small war raged inside his head, while a train was passing through the battleground. He must be hallucinating from the pain of his headache, he thought, because he distinctly heard the rhythmic click-clack of its wheels.

Slowly he turned his head to one side. His vision cleared. He studied a wall made of thick planks with mortar between them. There were rough-hewn white shelves filled with books on the whitewashed wall. There was also a map of a coastline and ocean that looked very familiar, though he couldn't think clearly enough to identify it at the moment.

He moved tentatively and became aware of soft textures against his skin—comfortable, friendly textures. He smelled the sweet-spicy scent of a wood fire, and his ears picked up the crackle and pop of burning logs. The train continued to click-clack across his mental landscape, however, reminding him of the Chicago train stations where he had hawked household soaps as a boy. Any second now a cop would walk up and say, "You little jerk, get out of here! I'm not tellin' ya again!"

Douglas shut his eyes and frowned wearily. Why

couldn't the cop see that he needed the money? Why did he always have to give up his territory? Never again. Never again. He wished the sound of the train would stop.

It did. But he heard the cop walking toward him. Hey, he wanted to shout, send some goon from public works to fix that floor. It creaks. And hey, flat-foot, you walk like a girl.

"Just lay still and let the waking come slowly," a soft female voice said. "You're not hurt or anything; just a wee bit hung over from the drug. As soon as you can get up to reach it, I'll bring you a cup of hot tea. If you're a bit queasy, there's a small room with your own private facilities in the corner. I've provided you with all the comforts of home, Douglas."

The speaker's Scottish burr jolted his memory; so did the cool undertone in it. Worried and confused, he raised his hands to his face and rubbed vigorously. Then he turned his head toward the voice and opened his eyes.

A beautiful redhead stood a few feet away, her arms crossed casually over her chest. She was dressed in a bulky white sweater and a flowing peasant skirt of a rich yellow-and-black plaid. Embroidered white socks disappeared under the skirt's calf-length hem. On her feet were lace-up leather shoes, sturdy and worn looking.

Her chestnut hair hung in a long braid that draped over one shoulder, ending at her breasts. She watched him with stern, amber-colored eyes. Behind her he saw the train. It was a spinning wheel.

It was a tribute to her appeal that he noticed last of all that she was separated from him by the bars of a cell, *his* cell. Sam sat right outside it, whining with welcome and thumping his tail on the wooden floor.

Douglas lurched upright and swayed dizzily. He planted his hands beside him and looked down. He was sitting on a comfortable bed, long enough to suit his height and wide enough for his shoulders.

His legs were draped with a soft gray blanket. His pants had been traded for loose tan corduroys, and when he glanced at his arms he realized that he now wore a dark blue sweater of incredibly soft wool.

"Who changed my clothes?" he muttered. "I feel like a Ken doll on Barbie's Terrorist Adventure."

"Don't be ungrateful, Mr. Kincaid. I've saved your finery for you. You'll get it back eventually. Now how about that cup of tea?"

He stared at her groggily. Then all of his frustration exploded in a weak roar. "Who the hell are you? What do you want with me? Where am I?"

"You're in jail in a pretty stone cottage tucked away in the loveliest mountains in the whole world, Douglas. You have your own facilities with running water and everything—all the modern conveniences—and a cozy bed. I'll keep you well fed and safe; if you're specially good, I'll even give you a bottle of your favorite Scotch whisky to soothe your poor hurt feelings. No harm will come to you, I swear."

She tapped one hand on a little wooden table that was pushed up against the cell bars. On a level with its top was a horizontal opening in the bars, just large enough to accommodate the passage of small items or plates of food. "I'll set your tea right here. You reach through and get it. That's how we'll deal with each other, Douglas. Don't expect me to get close enough for you to cause mischief.

"And you can't escape. The walls around you are two-feet thick, and made of stone. The window has been filled in with stone and mortar." She gestured toward the cell door. "It can't be jimmied, and I won't ever open it, not for any reason. Now, what do you take in your tea?"

"Blood. Yours, preferably."

"Tsk, tsk. I know you're not feeling well. You'll calm down—"

"The hell I will." He staggered off the bed and nearly fell before he reached the bars. She stepped back as he threw himself against the metal grid and

shook it with both hands. Nausea assailed him, and he leaned against the bars, panting.

"You're a fighter," she said with approval. "But then, you're of the Kincaid clan. I expect no less."

What kind of nonsense was that? He had no clan. He wasn't Scottish. He wasn't even sure he was human at the moment. "You can do anything you want to me, but you'll never get any money. And my people will hunt you down. You'll wish to God that you'd never heard of Douglas Kincaid."

"I already wish that. I'm not interested in ransom. But we'll talk about my interests later. You look a wee bit pale, Douglas. Best trot yourself to the facilities, because if you throw up out here, you'll be cleaning the floor. Unless you want to live in your own stink. That'd suit me fine too."

"I'm not going to take this!"

"Are you listening to me, Douglas? You don't have a choice."

His head throbbed. Cold sweat trickled down his back. He had no doubt that she meant what she said—her expression was totally composed. He almost admired her courage. He must be going insane.

He wrapped his hands tighter around the bars, raised a sock-clad foot, and kicked the table. It skidded across the floor and crashed into a large stone fireplace. His captor screeched, but it was a sound of anger, not fear. She grabbed a slender piece of kindling from the hearth, leapt forward with a speed that his dull reflexes couldn't parry, and rapped his knuckles like a ferocious schoolmarm.

Douglas jerked his smarting hands out of her range and stared at her in amazement. They both stood with legs braced, chests moving swiftly, eyes locked in challenge. She shook the stick at him. "Don't make it a war, Douglas. You'll lose."

"I never lose."

"Do you have any idea where you are?"

"It's either Scotland or a very bad nightmare."

"It's both, for the likes of you."

He swung about and stared at the map on his wall. Then he uttered an oath more appropriate to a street kid than an elegant billionaire. Colored in red were several thousand acres along a remote section of the Scottish coast.

"That's the property I'm buying," he noted, frowning.

He didn't have to look more closely to know that marked on the enormous section of land was the coastal village of Druradeen, with its quaint stone houses and postcard-perfect views, and that a few miles inland was stately MacRoth Hall, home of Angus MacRoth, the now-deceased Scottish laird.

MacRoth had owned everything—the village, the farms around it, the whisky distillery north of town—everything worth owning. The locals had paid annual dues to the old laird. They were all, in effect, tenants, or more precisely, modern-day peasants. Douglas planned to give them plenty of time to find new homes.

"That's the property you *were* buying," his captor corrected. "The deal won't go through without your signature. And there's only a month left on your purchase deadline."

Douglas turned around, clutching his aching head with one hand and his queasy stomach with the other. Confused, he stared at her. "How do you know about all this? And what concern is it to you?"

"Let's just say that I'm to make certain that the purchase deadline passes and the land goes to Angus MacRoth's next of kin."

"This is a travesty."

"No, this is a kidnapping, Douglas. Until your purchase deadline passes and the MacRoth lairdship goes to its rightful owners, you and I are going to live here together in peaceful seclusion."

"You've been sniffing the heather too much, doll. As soon as I get my bearings, we'll negotiate for my release."

Her chilling, disdainful gaze swept over him. "For once in your life, Douglas Kincaid, you can't negotiate, or buy, or charm your way into getting what you want." She smiled sweetly. "Now have some tea, won't you?"

He shook his head, felt even more sick, then staggered to the door in the corner of his cell. As he stepped into the confines of his tiny bathroom he heard her chuckling.

Elgiva sat by the fireplace in a large chair filled with colorful pillows, her head tilted back on the thick wood, her hands open and still on the armrests. She was exhausted, sad, and worried.

She couldn't take her eyes off of Douglas Kincaid, who lay sprawled on his bed asleep, one foot dangling as if he were perfectly relaxed. He had come out of the bathroom eventually, gone straight to the table she'd replaced at his cell bars, and shoved the cup of tea onto the floor.

He had smiled victoriously when the delicate old cup cracked open. Tea had splashed across a faded tapestry rug, worn but still beautiful. He had nodded with pleasure. Then without a word he had stretched out on his bed and immediately gone to sleep, as if his situation were a petty annoyance not worth discussing.

You'll drink my tea, she vowed silently, gritting her teeth. *And before I'm done with you, you'll learn to be civil and listen.*

Still, he reminded her of Jonathan, and that brought the worries. Jonathan would have been unconquerable in a situation such as this. Of course, her husband's strength had been of a quieter brand, a shy kind where women had been concerned. And he had been gentle and good humored, a big, sweet ox of a man, not a quick-tempered wolf like Kincaid.

She rose wearily and went to the cottage's front room, where she set a pot of beef stew to simmer on a small gas stove. Stuck here in the highlands with only the electricity from a gas-run generator—and that only to work the well pump—Elgiva longed for the bare comforts of her little apartment over her clothing shop in Druradeen. Without the stove, the gas heater in the other room, and the oil lamps hanging from the ceiling beams, life here would have been a bit too rustic.

Of course, she and Rob had grown up in worse, living in a crofter's cottage as outcasts from Angus MacRoth's hearth. He had treated them as if they were strangers, not his kin, his brother's orphans. He didn't care if the other MacRoths despised him for turning his back on his nearest blood; Angus had never asked for the love of his kinspeople or his tenants, even when many of them were one and the same.

Douglas Kincaid's dog padded into the room and nuzzled her hand. The unexpected comfort weakened her defenses, and tears stung her eyes. After she set Kincaid free, she'd have to go into hiding. It might be years before he stopped searching for her. He was the kind of man who would crave revenge. No matter. She'd run, if she had to, and leave the MacRoth holdings in Rob's control.

Rob would make a good laird. He wanted to write his historical novel, not manage an estate, but as the other rightful heir, it was his duty. Elgiva had been the best candidate to lead the kidnapping. Douglas Kincaid had an eye for the ladies. A woman might win his cooperation.

The evening wind whipped around the shingled eaves outside. Elgiva gazed wistfully through a small window set deep in the stone wall. A vista of craggy, heathered moor spread into the distance, with thick forests and clear, deep streams skirting its hollows.

They were shadowy and wild, these moors, and it was no wonder that the old ones still believed that they were populated by beautiful fairies and shaggy brownies, mischievous elves and merry fauns. The Good People, such as they were called, could be very helpful. She loved their legends and the heritage that had birthed them; she loved her country, and she loved the land that had belonged to her clan for seven centuries.

Elgiva craned her head anxiously when she heard movement from Kincaid's cell. She hurried back into the big room. He sat on the edge of his bed, staring angrily at the floor. His dog trotted to the cell and sat down as close as he could, pushing against the bars.

The big, sweet dog considers Kincaid a saint, Elgiva noted. But it didn't mean that he was one.

She went to her own bed, a large oak antique with angels carved into the headboard, set in the corner across from the fireplace. She sank slowly onto bright quilts covering a plump feather mattress. Then she clasped her hands in her lap and simply waited to see what would happen next.

Douglas Kincaid swung his head toward her. He scanned her from head to foot with narrowed, mocking eyes. "Do you have a name?" he asked sharply. "Or should I just call you whatever comes to mind? I can think of several unpleasant choices, at the moment."

"I'm sure you can. For my part, I'll call you what suits you best. Braggart. Show-off. Thief."

"Don't forget 'Innocent.' I haven't done anything illegal or immoral."

"It's not immoral to take what isn't yours?"

"I wanted a home in Scotland! Angus MacRoth offered to sell me a home. I don't understand why his heirs would protest. As soon as I sign the agreement, they'll get one million pounds. That's a lot of MacMoney."

"The money won't go to them. Angus willed it to the Bank of Scotland."

"Why would he do a pointless thing like that?"

"Because he was a hateful old man who liked to hurt people. Angus's heirs don't want the money, anyhow. They want their homes and their lives left in peace. You're planning to kick everyone out."

"I simply want my privacy. I'll *pay* to help everyone relocate."

"And close the village down? What would you do with the village?"

"I won't get rid of the village. It's cute."

"It's not cute! It's home!"

"It's got potential. I might build a hotel there; put in a golf course—"

"We don't play golf! We fish for a living, and raise sheep, and farm, and run little shops, and go to church, and send our children to school, and—"

"Tourists play golf," he said in exasperation. "Tourists bring money."

"Tourists come to gawk! They make the locals feel like actors in an amusement park!"

"Any country that has the Loch Ness monster is already an amusement park, as far as I'm concerned. Legends are worth a fortune on the open market, and this country is crawling with 'em."

Elgiva hummed an old tune and reached over to her spinning wheel. She wrapped one finger around the bobbin thread. "I have wound you with my strongest work, Douglas. I have you prisoner. I'll keep you prisoner. I'll let you go the day after your sneaky little option is up. By law, a laird's unclaimed estate goes to his nearest heirs. MacRoth Hall is by rights their home!"

"And I'll be very, very good to it. I'm going to put in a swimming pool and a helicopter pad."

Years of anger welled up inside her, along with a reckless urge to tell Douglas Kincaid sad stories he wouldn't care to hear. Elgiva went to the hearth and pulled a black cape from its peg by the fireplace. "I'm going for a walk now. I'll be doing this every afternoon." She whipped the cape around her and fastened it at her throat.

"I hope you like beef stew, Douglas. Can you smell it simmering on the stove? We'll have supper just as soon as I get back. You can break your bowl on the floor. What fun! Come along, dog."

Kincaid jumped up and threw himself at the bars, grabbing them and jerking viciously. The violent power of his body and hands was an unnerving sight. "Who are you?" he yelled. "What personal stake do you have in this?"

As she strode from the room with his dog at her heels, she called calmly, "Angus MacRoth stole from his own kin, Douglas. His holdings will go back to his heirs, and there'll be naught you can do about it. No Scottish court will heed your protests."

"I'll own that land, and I'll own *you*!"

Elgiva shivered. She had read that Douglas Kincaid never made idle threats.

Douglas prowled his cell. He shoved the table and chair aside so that he could pace. When he heard the heavy door creak open in the outer room of the cottage, he stepped to the bars and gazed out with pure animosity.

His kidnapper swept into view, her cheeks rosy from the cold, the magnificent black cape swirling around her. The sight was so affecting that he couldn't speak for a moment—damn her, she was incredible to look at, and the spirit that gleamed in those golden eyes drew him despite his fury. Sam, tongue lolling, bounded over to the cell without the least bit of shame.

"Sam, you damned traitor," Douglas accused, but stroked his head.

" 'Sam,' is it?" the woman asked. "Good! I'll call him *Shom*. Short for *Shomhairle*. That's the Gaelic form of Samuel." She clapped her hands. "You're a good Scottish dog now, Shom!"

Sam thumped his tail as if he understood. Douglas glared from him to the woman. "You left without giving me a chance to ask more questions," he protested. "Coward."

"I thought you needed a wee bit of privacy to mull things over." She shrugged the cape off and hung it on a wooden peg beside the hearth. "Besides, I had a fierce need for my evening stroll. The moors called to me."

"They probably said, 'Run for your life. You're in deep trouble.' "

She shrugged, but he was surprised to see her shoulders slump a little. "So be it."

"Are you ever going to tell me your name?"

"No." She fluffed her long plaid skirt then knelt on the stone hearth to stir up the fire. "I'll not make it easier for you to track me after you're set free. Your hired hounds will sniff out my identity quick enough."

"What keeps you from just murdering me?" he asked nonchalantly. "Wouldn't that be simpler than keeping me—rather, *trying* to keep me—penned up for a month?"

"Aye. If I were an evil person. But I won't be turned into a killer, even by the disgusting likes of you. So rest easy."

"And I suppose that you won't explain how you managed to crash my New Year's Eve party and carry me off without getting caught."

"I have a drop or two of fairy blood. I enchanted you and spirited you away. Don't be surprised if the world seems different when I send you back from *Elf-hame*."

"*Elf-hame?*"

"Elf home. The kingdom of the Good People."

She smiled at the dancing fire, and shivers ran up Douglas's spine. He thought again of her power over his senses back in New York. He watched Sam, who lay near her on a hearth rug, looking content. Enchanted? *Get a grip on yourself, Kincaid.*

"You're the biggest fairy I've ever seen," he noted, and made sure it didn't sound like a compliment. "But then, with your height, you can carry so much extra weight."

She twisted to study him with stern eyes. "You didn't seem to think I was too much for you back in New York."

"I was hoping for a one-night stand. You looked easy. Big and easy. Six feet of easy."

Even in the shadowy firelight he could see her face tighten. "I'm not too big for a *real* man," she retorted. "Nor *easy*, you slobbering cretin. And I'm a perfectly respectable weight for my height."

"Oh? You must wear four-inch spikes when you step on the scales."

She smiled thinly and stabbed a poker into the fire. "It's not wise to insult the person who'll be bringing your meals to you. The *only* person who'll look after you."

"Your co-conspirators wouldn't want me starved, I'm sure."

"There's only me, Douglas. It was a one-woman plot. I'm the self-appointed representative of the people who stand to lose if you take over Angus MacRoth's holdings."

"Don't waste your breath telling me a fairy tale. One person working alone couldn't have circumvented my security people. They're the best. In fact, they're probably halfway to finding this little torture nest of yours already.

"No one but my executive staff will ever know that I'm missing. You and your pals will be hunted down by experts who make government investigators look like Boy Scouts. You and everyone who helped you will end up in American prisons for the rest of your lives. If you'd like to know what'll happen to you there, I'll be glad to go into detail."

"Shush, Douglas, you're sounding like a character in one of those silly gangster movies you watch all the time. 'Come out with your hands up, or I'll send Father O'Brien in to get you!' Threaten all your want. It's no difference to me. But there's only me to hate. Maybe you'll get tired of your ranting and speak to me as a gentleman would."

She stood, shot him a baleful look, then stretched languidly, as if taunting him. Under her bulky white sweater her breasts rose with magnificent effect.

The flowing skirt clung to her tapering stomach and the proportioned flair of her hips. Douglas knew that many men must have told this woman how beautiful her curves were, and his petty insults hadn't bothered her a bit.

"Look, doll, if I'm going to be stuck with you for a while, at least make up a name. Otherwise I'll make up my own. And I don't think you'll appreciate it."

"All right. Fair enough." She clasped her hands behind her and rocked back and forth, thinking. After a minute she told, "Your Ladyship will do nicely."

Douglas growled in frustration. "Jumbo," he announced, then nodded with satisfaction. "Jumbo. It's perfect. Bring me some dinner, Jumbo. Waddle as fast as you can."

She glowered at him for a moment, then sighed. "Are you nearly starving, you poor man?"

"I could eat. It's been at least a day since I had anything, in case you've forgotten."

She went to the other room and returned a minute later with two bowls of stew but only one spoon. "Poor, poor Douglas." She set one bowl on the floor for an eagerly waiting Sam. Then she carried the other one to her chair by the hearth and began to eat.

Douglas scowled at her. "Very funny. I said I'm hungry."

"You were speaking to some fat phantom named Jumbo, not to myself."

"You wouldn't let me go hungry out of spite, would you?"

She put a succulent-looking spoonful of beef and carrots into her mouth and savored it for a long time before she swallowed. "Apologize," she ordered calmly. "Or do without supper."

"To hell with it." He lay down on his bed and flipped the blanket over his legs. "Good night, Jumbo."

"Starve because of your bad temper, Kincaid." Above the sound of his stomach grumbling, Douglas heard her soft, infuriating laughter.

* * *

Elgiva couldn't help herself. She edged closer until she was near enough to reach through the bars if she wanted and touch Kincaid as he slept.

From a window near the fireplace a long block of morning sunshine poured across the cottage, bathing his chest and stopping short of his face. He had wrenched his sweater up during the night, and his blanket lay around his knees.

Hot-blooded he was, like all of his Kincaid ancestors, Elgiva thought. Black-haired and dark-eyed the legends said; the men of the clan had been lordly, handsome warriors with a reputation for stealing the prettiest women from their rival clans. She and Douglas Kincaid most likely shared a bloodline, in some distant and convoluted way.

She moved an inch more. She had dared fate in a similiar fashion as a child, when, during a family picnic by the ocean, she had explored the windcarved cliffs of Arragowan. She had heard that each time the surf pulled back, a brave watcher could peek down and see *An Uamh Ghabhach*, the Danger Cave.

In 1417 her ancestor Malcolm MacRoth had been cornered there by a dozen Kincaid swordsmen. During the centuries since, the sea had crept closer to the cave, hiding it. Legend said that anyone who could glimpse the place in modern times would see Malcolm MacRoth's ghost fighting the spectres of the Kincaids.

She had wanted so badly to see that. Her horrified parents had found her stretched half-over the cliff's edge, craning her neck to watch the rocks below the surf.

Now she had a Kincaid to watch in the flesh, and she felt as she had when she was six, her heart pounding with fear and elation, her body refusing to move from a place of danger, her instincts telling her against reason that she would be all right.

Elgiva gazed at his exposed stomach, and she was

mesmerized by the slow rise and fall of hard masculine muscles furred with black hair. A streak of silver hair grew down the center of it, disappearing under the waistband of his trousers like a guideline to his navel and parts beyond. It was definitely silver, not gray, and very attractive.

Elgiva pressed her face between the bars, her eyes searching the thick hair on his head. There was no silver there, but perhaps he dyed his hair. No, she decided, recalling that he was only thirty-seven years old. Only three years older than herself. One of the youngest billionaires in the world. Certainly one of the least lonely ones, considering what she'd read about his ladyfriends.

Almost all had been blondes. Small, delicate blondes. That was why she'd worn a blond wig to his party. She hadn't been able to fake the small and delicate part, of course, but she'd won his attention anyway. Apparently, when Douglas Kincaid was in great need, any blonde in a low-cut gown would do.

Feeling absurdly hurt, she turned her back. The dog came up, dipped his muzzle into the pocket of her long white robe, and snuffled for the piece of biscuit she'd hidden there. He and she had already developed this game of hide-and-seek. What a wonderful, intelligent animal he was, and so loving. How could a man such as Douglas Kincaid deserve him? Elgiva leaned against the bars and distractedly watched Shom munch his treat.

By the time she registered the creak and bump behind her as the sound of Kincaid launching his large body from the bed, it was too late to escape. One of his arms stabbed through the bars and circled her neck.

Elgiva shrieked with fury and struggled, clawing at his arm and then trying to elbow him, a tactic which backfired because she smashed her elbow into the bars. Pain shot up her arm.

"Stop it, Jumbo," he commanded loudly. "Or I'll squeeze you until your eyes pop."

Despite the threat, his grip was tight but not painful. Elgiva forced herself to be still and breathe normally. "You won't get anything for your mischief. If you strangle me, you'll still be trapped. And there's naught you can do to make me open the cell door."

"Unless you've got the keys on you."

"Would I be such a fool?"

"You kidnapped one of the most powerful men in the world. I'd say you rank right up there with the major fools of all time."

"Faith! What glory you give yourself!"

"Let's see if I'm right."

She yelped with anger when his other hand reached around her and clasped her hip. He exposed the pocket where she'd hidden Sam's treat. "Great, Sam," he muttered. "Thanks for the slobber." He casually wiped his fingers on the front of her robe, just below the thick belt.

"Frumpy," Douglas Kincaid taunted, his breath warm on her neck. "I liked the green dress better." He drew a finger back and forth.

Elgiva's belly shrank from the pressure, and she breathed faster. "Go ahead and enjoy yourself, Douglas. It'll be the last good time you have."

"Do you always threaten your kidnap victims?" he asked. Then he untied the belt. "I can't reach your other pocket," he explained.

"There is no other pocket. Just the one."

"Just one kidnapper. Just one pocket. I tend to distrust anything you say." He jerked the far side of her robe across her belly and groped the material, searching for the pocket. When he found it he chuckled ruefully and dug his hand into the opening.

But all he withdrew was a small photograph in a hard plastic cover. He held it up. "Looks like a pro linebacker wearing a kilt. Someone ought to tell the crayon people about his hair color. That's the brightest red I've ever seen. Who is this monster?"

Elgiva shut her eyes, aching inside. She had slipped Jonathan's picture into her pocket for inspiration.

He'd tried so hard to hide his disappointment with life. The least she could do for his memory was triumph over this man who had the kind of money and prestige Jonathan had always coveted.

But here she stood with Douglas Kincaid's strong arm around her throat, her robe undone, his hot, amused breath on her neck, and his provocative masculine scent seeping into her senses—unwashed, brutal, yet still tinged with the essence of a fine cologne.

"Who is he?" Kincaid demanded again, jerking her lightly.

"My husband. But he's dead. Two years dead. Put the picture back."

"Oh, no. This could be very helpful. I'll give it to my people when they find me. Which should be soon."

She flashed a hand out and snapped the picture from his unsuspecting fingers, then twirled it to a safe spot on the floor. "Think again, Mr. Kincaid."

He whistled. "Sam! Fetch!"

Obediently the big retriever went to the photograph and, after some maneuvering, got it into his mouth. Elgiva watched in despair. "Shom! No!"

The dog hesitated, watching them both anxiously, the photograph protruding from his mouth like a plastic tongue. "Sam! Come!" Kincaid called. Sam started forward.

"Shom! Stay!" Elgiva shouted. He stopped.

"Come!"

"Stay, beastie, stay!"

"Sam! *Now!*" Kincaid gestured to one side.

"Shom, please, Shom."

The dog whined sadly but trotted to the cell and deposited the photograph on the floor between the bars. He licked Elgiva's hand then sat down, huffing in bewilderment. "It's all right, poor beastie," she whispered hoarsely. "You have to obey your brute master, I know."

"If only it were that easy with you," the brute grumbled.

She twisted against the corded strength of his arm. "You see that I haven't got the key to the cell. Now let me go. Remember that I'm your only link to food and heat. Be a noble captive, Douglas. You'll get as good as you give, that I promise."

"Oh? I'll expect this, then." His hand delved under the robe, flattening across her midsection. Elgiva's harshly indrawn breath made a loud rasping sound in the quiet cottage, and he chuckled with victory. "If the linebacker in a skirt *is* your late husband, which I doubt, did you wear these kind of feed sacks to bed with him?"

"This is a sensible gown, meant for keeping the highland chill from giving me pneumonia."

"There are better ways to keep warm, Jumbo." His hand cupped her navel, and his big, blunt forefinger began to trace a circle around it. "You could have gotten a lot more help out of me the other night if you'd used a different strategy." His voice was low and rumbling. "Who knows? By now you might have persuaded me to do anything you want, whatever it is you *really* want."

"You're a liar, Douglas. I've studied you enough to know you'd never be a fool for love."

He laughed heartily, while his hand rose by slow degrees up her stomach. "Did you think I was look-ing for *love* the other night? You're a sentimental criminal, for damned sure."

Elgiva clutched his free arm with both of hers. Despite her fierce downward pressure, his hand con-tinued to rise. "Don't do this," she said between gritted teeth.

"What? This?" He curved his palm under her right breast, molding the heavy nightgown to the already oversensitized skin. Slowly his thumb settled on the tip of her nipple. "Why, Jumbo, that's an alert little beastie you've got there."

She dug her fingernails into his wrist. His arm jostled her neck enough to remind her that she was still held tightly. Elgiva groaned in pure fury. "You'll pay for this, you nasty spawn of Kincaid."

"It'll be worth it. A man *ought* to be punished for enjoying himself this much without the least bit of guilt."

"I'm sure that's a familiar attitude for you." Her breath broke in her lungs as his hand went to her other breast, squeezing gently. She shivered when he took the rigid nipple between his thumb and forefinger and rubbed it. It tightened even more under his care.

"Why, Jumbo, is this the Loch Ness monster?" he asked coyly. "Or are you just glad to see me?"

"You can't shame me with your lecherous pawing," she whispered, stomping the floor in frustration.

"I'll have to try harder, then. Oh! Look what I found on the feed sack! Buttons!" His fingers were nimble as they unfastened the white stoneware buttons that ran from beneath her breasts to her throat. "How prim. Are you sure you're the same woman who nearly fogged my mirror?" He dipped his hand inside her gown, and Elgiva cried out in dismay.

"I don't understand you," he whispered gruffly. His hand trailed from one turgid peak to the other, exploring with an unexpected tenderness that was maddening. "This is not the reaction of a woman who doesn't want me to touch her."

She was shaking, so embarrassed and confused that she could barely keep her teeth from chattering. "I can't help what a man's touch does to me! It's of no consequence under the circumstances!"

"Stop pretending, Jumbo," he ordered, but there was a note of bewilderment in his voice. "Tell me what you really want from me."

"I want you to go back to America and trouble me no more!"

"Why are you risking your future for a stupid scheme?" He loosened his grip on her neck a little. His free hand lay still over her heart, the fingers between her breasts. "Are *you* the heir who'll get everything of MacRoth's if I don't buy it?" He drew a sharp breath. "Of course! A greedy relative! I should have known!"

"That's not the way it is!"

"Do you honestly think you can kidnap me, coerce me, then blithely go free, a happy heiress, the lady of the estate?"

She put her hands to her forehead, shut her eyes, and laughed wearily. "You can't understand. I'm doing this for the MacRoth heritage, not myself. It doesn't matter what happens to me."

To her amazement, he let her go. His hand slid up from her breasts to hold her chin, though not in a harsh grip. Trembling violently, Elgiva turned around and, as his hand seared her skin, stared up at him. His dark eyes swept over her face in angry assessment.

"I don't believe in fairy tales," he said grimly.

"Then don't listen to them. Listen to your heart. Maybe it's the same thing."

"I'll listen when you let me out of here. Do it now and I'll be a reasonable man. I swear it."

"You mean you'll be 'reasonable' by your own terms. No. Too much is at stake." She stepped back quickly.

"You're undoubtedly the MacRoth heir. What's your first name?"

"Slugger. Don't try anything again, or I'll live up to it."

He pounded one fist against the bars. "You can't keep me here for a month! I have deals underway all over the world! I can't stay holed up in this godforsaken place!"

Without his hands on her any longer, calm began to return. Elgiva eyed him firmly. "Your most important work is right here. Now eat your breakfast. I'm sure it's cold."

She gestured toward the table by the serving window. On it sat two platters filled with food—fried eggs, sausages, pancakes, blueberry scones, and biscuit bread. There was handsome silverwave, a cloth napkin, and an insulated coffeepot filled to the brim. She had even taken the risk of giving him another beautiful old cup.

"You're an unusual kidnapper," he said, sounding troubled.

"I don't mean you any harm. I keep telling you that. Which is more than you can say to me."

He studied her for a moment. His stomach rumbled loudly. As if on cue he and she both glanced down at the photograph that lay at his feet. Elgiva held her breath as he picked it up.

"It's truly my husband, and he's truly dead," she murmured. "He wasn't a MacRoth. Don't keep his picture out of spite."

"Here."

When he held it through the bars, she advanced cautiously, gauging his intentions. But if his expression was troubled, it was also calm for the first time. She took the photograph from him and tucked it back into the pocket of her robe. Then she said something she never thought she'd say to Douglas Kincaid.

"Thank you."

"You left my family pictures in my wallet. Thank *you.*"

His kindness, no matter how fleeting or reluctant, was so affecting that tears came to her eyes. Mortified by his power over her emotions, Elgiva hurried into the front room, shutting the door behind her. Shaking, she stripped, then stood naked in the little stall in one corner and took the only kind of shower the water tank could provide—ice-cold. It was much needed.

Three

Douglas woke with a start, his mind still tuned to a potently erotic dream about his captor. In it she opened the door of his cell and came to his bed, naked, warm, seething with needs that only he could satisfy. And despite the open door all he could think about was reaching for her, stroking her, pulling her down beside him onto the narrow bed. He didn't want to leave.

Douglas shook that foolish idea aside and squinted into the afternoon sunlight. Gold-eyes was gone; the fire burned low on the hearth, and Sam was sound asleep on a rug nearby, snoring.

No wonder. She had fed Sam a huge meal at lunch, too, and she was a fantastic cook. Afterward she'd worked at her spinning wheel, and the rhythmic clicking of the treadle had been as hypnotizing as a metronome. Douglas had lain on the bed on his stomach, facing her, too stubborn to start a conversation, but secretly eager to watch her as she worked.

Occasionally she had smiled in his direction, but she seemed no more willing to discuss their outrageous situation than he was. Lulled by the sound of her spinning wheel, a full stomach, the crackling fire, and a feeling that bordered on stoic acceptance of his fate, he had fallen asleep.

Now he ruefully patted his stomach. She was stuffing him on purpose to keep him lazy and content, like a fat lion caged at a zoo. Boredom and confinement would make it easy to fall into her plan. Douglas shook his head. He'd look like Orson Welles unless he got out of there soon. *And he would get out soon.*

T. S. Audubon was probably on the verge of finding him already. Audubon was not only a longtime personal friend, but he also was the best executive-protection expert in the world.

And what then? Douglas asked himself, frowning. Capture Gold-eyes and her cronies? Definitely. Find out the true nature of their scheme? Certainly. Try to have the whole bunch extradited to America and send them to prison for the rest of their Scottish lives? He hesitated.

Out of bed now and moving restlessly around the small cell, Douglas wondered if it was foolish to be swayed by the MacRoth woman's story about ancestral homes and desperate tenants. But there was a sincerity about her, an uncluttered idealism, that disturbed him. Was he really going to hurt people by buying the estate? Did it mean more to them than he realized?

He shook his head. He had not built a three-billion-dollar fortune by being indecisive and soft hearted. His father had been both, and had suffered for it. In business Douglas had established a reputation for generosity, honesty, and superb management, but also for toughness. No matter how much Gold-eyes intrigued him, he wouldn't give her what she wanted, and he wouldn't let her get away scot-free.

Douglas corrected himself grimly. *Scot*-free.

Elgiva walked against the cold January wind, her head bowed and her hooded cape held tight against her body. Several miles from the cottage, after crossing ridges and woodland, she came to the shores of Loch Talrigh. The northern tip of the great inland lake was surrounded by steep mountains covered with firs. The air was calm; the mountains held the wind at bay. The water was deep and so black that it had a purple tint.

In the center was a craggy island. And on the island, nearly consuming every foot of the rock, were the ruins of Castle Talrigh. Elgiva tossed her hood back and stood on the shore studying the mighty old place. Then she searched the water's edge and, after a moment of careful exploration with the toes of her rubber boots, found the stone causeway a few inches under the water.

The walk across to the castle took a long time, because the ancient causeway zigzagged and one had to look carefully to find its path. Many a warrior had discovered himself and his horse swimming in the loch while the castle's defenders rained arrows or, later, musket fire on him. Many of her own ancestors had died that way, in fact.

When she reached the brooding fortress she went into a crumbling courtyard and sat down on a pile of stone blocks. The winter sun cast long shadows. She had come here to think about Douglas, but she didn't have much time before dark.

Yes, she decided finally, this place was where she should begin his education. She'd show him photographs and try to condense seven hundred years of Kincaid history into a pretty little package that wouldn't bore him. After she set him free perhaps he'd care enough to come here and see *his* ancestral home firsthand.

Perhaps the majesty of it would touch him as nothing else could, and he'd understand why she'd taken him prisoner to preserve her own heritage. Then again, after he learned what it meant to be a Kincaid, he might seek revenge on her with even greater delight.

She thought for a while longer, then decided upon her plan. She would tell him his family history but avoid explaining why Castle Talrigh, ancient clan seat of the Kincaids, had been destroyed.

She most definitely would not tell him by whom.

T. S. Audubon had been twenty-one years old in the summer of 1971, a summer that he'd spent trying to survive in the jungles of Vietnam. He had been one of the toughest, smartest, and most respected sergeants in his battalion, but he wouldn't be alive now except for the bravery that summer of an eighteen-year-old corporal named Douglas Kincaid.

The hard-nosed Chicago kid had carried his wounded sergeant to safety through a hail of enemy fire. Blood had been streaming down Kincaid's face from a shrapnel wound. The fact that Kincaid was belting out an off-key rendition of "God Bless America" at the time always lent the memory a special drama to Audubon.

Their wartime friendship had grown over the next two decades, as Douglas's brilliance and ambition shot him to the top of the moneyed world that Audubon had inhabited since birth. They shared a love for the good things in life, a flair for the dramatic, and an innate idealism.

Within an hour after Douglas was discovered missing, Audubon set the awesome expertise of his fifty-member team to work on finding him.

They were now a little closer to doing that. As he shook hands with the ruddy-faced little man seated at the table in Druradeen's pub, Audubon's sixth sense told him that the village's mayor would lie at the drop of a tam-o'-shanter. The man was too pleased to see him.

"State your business, Mr. Audubon," Duncan MacRoth said, smiling. "The sheriff over in Terkleshire called to say you'd be by. Something about a local woman you're looking to find."

"Yes." Audubon laid a sheet of paper on the table. "See this emblem? The griffin and the rams? I was told that it's the crest of the MacRoth clan."

"Aye, and a bonnie one it is."

"The woman I'm looking for was wearing a piece of jewelry with this emblem on it at a party last week. In America. New York City, to be exact."

"Folks here don't travel too much. They're lucky to get down to Edinburgh once a year, much less to America. What are you needing this woman for?"

"I'm a private investigator. She's involved with a client of mine. She's a tall woman, and very well built, if you understand my meaning. Early thirties. Very pretty. With blond hair—a wig, I suspect."

"Faith! I'd remember if we had such a woman in this village! She doesn't sound familiar."

"Oh? I understand that Elgiva MacRoth, who runs a little sweater shop down the street here, fits my description. Except that she has dark reddish-brown hair. Her shop is closed. I was told she was on vacation. Could you tell me where?"

"Oh! Elgiva! Well, she's away in . . . uhmmm, let's see . . . Florida. Yes. Perhaps she did go to America. To Disney World. That's right." The mayor beamed and nodded. The hard glitter in his eyes told Audubon that he didn't give a damn if anyone believed him. It was his story, and he was going to stick to it.

"An interesting choice."

Mayor MacRoth shrugged gracefully. "She has unusual interests, that Elgiva. Niece of the laird, you see. And old Angus was an eccentric."

"She's wealthy, then? One of the laird's heirs?"

"Oh, she's not wealthy. Angus was a mean bastard. Treated her and her brother worse than beggars. But she and her husband put a wee bit of money away over the years. They had no children to spend it on, poor folks. He was a fisherman. Drowned in a storm—"

"She has a brother?" Audubon asked impatiently.

"Aye. He's a fisherman too. And a writer, on the side. Not published yet, though. But a fine, fine, man—"

"Could you tell me where he is?"

"Disney World," a feisty voice interjected.

Audubon looked up to find a grandmotherly little woman watching him from the pub's door. "Disney World," she repeated firmly, and snapped the jacket lapels of her sturdy dress suit for emphasis. "To see those mice. Mickey and Minnie. Yes. They're kin of ours, you know."

"Mickey and Minnie?" Audubon asked dryly.

"Elgiva and Rob, and don't you be saucy to me, lad," she retorted.

"I apologize."

"This is Mr. Audubon, Mother," the mayor said. "Would you happen to have heard when Elgiva and Rob might be coming back home?"

"Oh, not for weeks! They were going on to that other famous American place. Hmmm . . . Tara. Yes! They were going to see Tara."

Audubon looked from the mayor to the mayor's mother. Both smiled benignly. Now Audubon knew he was on the right track, but the track was getting crowded with more MacRoths than he'd ever expected.

"You've been as silent as the mountains all evening, Douglas. What's wrong?"

Elgiva watched him lounge in a big upholstered chair near his bed, his long legs crossed at the ankles, his strong-jawed face carved into mysterious patterns in the firelight. He could have lighted his lantern and read one of the books on his shelves. She'd given him two-dozen American novels, ones she assumed he'd like, with lots of sex and violence.

Or he could have worked crosswords in one of the many puzzle books she'd provided. She'd read that crossword puzzles were one of his favorite entertainments. When he couldn't think of the correct words, he made up better ones. Resourceful and creative, that was Douglas Kincaid, though not particular about the rules.

But all he did was scrutinize her. Elgiva lifted tense hands from the sweater she was knitting. Shom raised his golden head from her feet and looked around sleepily. "What's the matter, Douglas?" she asked again.

He chuckled, but it was more of a disgruntled growl than a sound of pleasure. "Nothing. I love being kidnapped." He lifted one large foot, which was covered in a bright red wool sock and a sandal of wide leather straps. "I feel like a Celtic Moonie."

"You've no need for real shoes. You won't be going outdoors."

He thumped his foot down and cursed softly. "I'll enjoy proving you wrong."

She sighed. Tonight was not the time to begin telling him about his Scotch heritage, it seemed. "In the wooden box under your bed you'll find a cassette player, Douglas, and a few dozen of your favorite tapes. All those jazz people you like so much. I put in some tapes of the great classics of the bagpipe as well. Why don't you listen to some ancient *ceol mor* to calm your nerves?"

"My nerves are still calm from dinner."

"You're welcome. I'm a grand cook."

"I wasn't saying thanks." He muttered something she could barely hear, something about her husband probably looking like someone named Pee-Wee Herman before she began to feed him. "Your husband," he repeated in a louder voice, speaking to her directly.

"Hmmm?" Elgiva forced her attention on her knitting needles and tried to appear nonchalant.

"Did he die of overeating?"

Elgiva told him grimly, "It's not gentlemanly to make fun of a widow's loss."

"It's not ladylike to shoot an innocent stranger in the butt with a tranquilizer dart."

"I liked you better when you weren't talking, Douglas."

"I liked you better when you were a blond sex machine."

"How about having another big piece of Madeira cake?"

"Stop trying to brainwash me with food."

"It's not brainwashing. It's hospitality."

"Did you learn hospitality from a terrorist?"

"You could make this a pleasant month, if you'd try."

"Give me that bottle of whisky you mentioned."

"Not tonight. Drinking might put you in an uglier mood."

"That's not possible."

"Be a good lad, Douglas, and *earn* the right to a nip of Scotland's best."

"Dammit!" He glared at her from the shadows of his corner like a predatory animal crouched in its cave, wanting to pounce on a victim. "You manipulative little—"

"Tsk, tsk, Douglas. I'm not a *little* anything. You said so yourself."

He was silent, momentarily outmaneuvered. Then his slow, wicked smile appeared. "So tell me, Jumbo, would you like to be fondled again? With a little creative positioning we could do anything you want, even through the bars." He held out his hands and wiggled the fingers lecherously. "Strip to your bare plaid, lassie, and come to your reward."

She jabbed herself with a knitting needle. Through gritted teeth she told him, "I'd give you better than you deserve."

"Prove it."

"Dream away, Douglas. You'd be spoiled for the rest, after having the best."

"I deserve the best. But in a smaller package, of course. And with blond hair—the real thing, not a cheap wig."

"You poor, poor bachelor. If you don't curb your temper you'll never find a wife to warm your icy soul."

"So tell me, Ann MacLanders, how long were you married?"

"Twelve years."

"All in a row? To the same unlucky man?"

She rolled her eyes. "Aye, brute. I know you can't understand loyalty such as that."

"Tell me, did you meet him at reform school?"

"No. We were promised as children."

After a stunned moment, Kincaid said, "Isn't that like shopping for Christmas in July?"

"It's a custom around here. The mothers plan the marriages for their bairns."

"Oh, come on, Jumbo, you're too modern for that."

"It's not a bad custom. My mother chose well. I could have broken the bonds, if I'd wanted. And he could have as well. But we decided that we could build a good home together."

"So you loved each other."

"We respected each other. That's more important."

He considered that information in silence, frowning. When he spoke again his voice was probing. "Then you had a happy marriage."

"It was a fine marriage."

"A *happy* marriage?"

She clenched her fists and demanded in exasperation. "What's it matter to you, Douglas?"

"You had an unhappy marriage," he concluded smugly. "I'm not surprised. You'd be too much trouble for most men."

"We had a good, decent marriage! Now stop your snooping!"

"Aren't there any baby Jumbos?"

"No!"

"Why not?"

"We couldn't have any!"

"Who couldn't? You or him?"

"Mind your own business."

"I was doing that until a few days ago. Now I'm being forced to play gossip monger just to keep myself entertained. So, was Mr. Jumbo shooting blanks? Or was he just afraid you'd hurt him in bed? I know—he didn't want to provoke any flashbacks from your days as a bar bouncer."

She vaulted to her feet, letting the knitting fall

unheeded to the hearth. "Stop it! Stop your cruel little picking!" Her voice broke. "You g–great, ugly, arrogant d–devil!"

He got to his feet also, frowning harder. "I was just giving a little of the same medicine—"

"Shut up!" Elgiva choked on the last word, and knew to her shame that she was about to cry in front of the heartless Douglas Kincaid, who'd undoubtedly get a laugh from it. She grabbed her cape from its peg. Shom scrambled to his feet, woofing softly.

"You can't be serious about going out," Kincaid protested, sounding perturbed. "It's freezing out there, and pitch-dark."

"It's more pleasant than in here."

Kincaid gestured to his dog. "Sam, follow!"

Elgiva headed for the front room. "I don't need—" she struggled with her voice—"I don't need—"

"You need," Douglas Kincaid interjected flatly, and he might have been talking about a lot more than Shom's protection. "Sam, go."

The big golden retriever stayed at Elgiva's heels as she hurried outside, slamming the cottage door. She took a deep breath of cold, reviving air, but couldn't stop the tears from sliding down her face.

She understood why Douglas Kincaid enjoyed tormenting her. Any proud fighter would look for vulnerable spots in his kidnapper's armor. She didn't understand, however, why she had let him find them so easily.

She had been gone for two hours, and the wind howled louder with every new minute. Douglas timed her with his diamond-studded wristwatch and chided himself for worrying about her well-being.

It occurred to him that she could easily have taken his watch when he was drugged. She must have realized that it was very valuable. But the watch, like the money that had been in his wallet, the pho-

tographs of his sister, brother, and parents, and his
jeweled car keys had not been stolen. He'd found
them in a small paper bag tucked among the clothes
she'd given him.

She's no thief.

In his cell's tiny bathroom she'd put his favorite
soap, shaving cream, and deodorant—even his favorite toothpaste. When she'd said that she wanted
him to have all the comforts of home, she'd meant
it.

His damned shower gave only cold water, but then,
so did hers. He'd heard her shower running in the
front room this morning, and when she'd returned
to the main room dressed in trousers and a sweater
he had seen the blue cast to her fair complexion.
She was suffering too.

Without complaining.

Douglas ran a hand down the front of his chest,
then dropped his troubled gaze to the neat ribs of a
soft gray sweater he wore with the gray trousers
she'd provided. He assumed that she'd made this
sweater herself.

For you, yes. And it's perfect.

Of course, her motivations were selfish. She wanted
to win his friendship. She'd need it, after he got out
of her trap.

Douglas checked his watch again. What in the hell
was she doing out on those empty moors? Why did
he care? Audubon would find him before long. But
in the meantime, where was she? He racked his
brain for information on the highlands. Weren't there
wolves up here?

It wouldn't hurt to be nice to her from now on.

Douglas went to the bars and shook them fiercely.
"Come back," he shouted. "If anything's going to eat
you alive, it's going to be me."

A few minutes later he heard her return. A draft of
winter wind filtered through the main room to his
cell, bringing with it the scents of the night and the
land. Sam trotted into the room, his tail wagging,

and came to the cell bars. Douglas stroked his cold fur and gazed hard at the open door to the front room, where he heard her moving about. Getting undressed? She ran water for a few minutes, not in the shower, he decided, but in a sink. He heard her splashing vigorously.

"I hope that's you," he called, "and not some badass brownie who broke in to case the joint."

She turned off the kerosene lamp in the front room and strode into his view wearing the long white robe bundled tightly around her. The linen night-gown shown under her chin, where a strip of white ribbon tied it shut. On her feet were bulky gray socks, probably from the same silver-gray breed of sheep who'd supplied the wool for his sweater.

Douglas felt the quick, uneven slamming of blood through his veins. Even wrapped in a ton of wool and linen she was arousing.

Her eyes glanced over him with disdain; stroking her wind-tangled hair, she knelt on the hearth. With her chestnut mane trailing down her back in turbulent rivers of gold and red, she began banking what remained of the night's fire.

"You must love to walk on the moors," he ventured politely.

"Good night, Mr. Kincaid." She finished with the fireplace and went to the heater near his cell. As she bent over the controls Douglas inhaled the scent of her body and hair. She smelled like the night wind, but also spicy, like wood smoke. Abruptly Douglas imagined himself surrounded by that intriguing fragrance, his face nuzzled into her hair, his body bathed in her scent through intimate contact.

She straightened, but the set of her shoulders conveyed fatigue or defeat; he wasn't sure which. "If you get too cold during the night, bang on the bars of the cell and wake me up," she told him in a clipped, formal tone. "I'll turn the heater up a wee bit."

"Listen, Goldie—"

"Goldie, is it?" She arched a brow.

"She's the woman who won't tell me her name."

"What happened to Jumbo?"

"She went for a walk and got eaten by a wolf. Or maybe a brownie ran off with her. I don't know. But I like Goldie better, anyway."

She made a weary, disgusted sound. "I know there's an insult in that somewhere, but I can't figure it out right now. Good night."

"Not an insult. An apology."

Her eyes flickered with surprise. "I didn't expect an apology. What does it mean?"

"In America the dictionary defines it as a request for forgiveness. What does it mean in Scotland?"

She sighed at his coyness. "Prisoners aren't supposed to apologize. In fact, in all I read about the great Kincaid, I never saw a reference to him apologizing for much of *anything*."

"Dammit, you're not making this easy. All I'm saying is that I'm sorry for insulting you and your late husband. Apology ended. Good night." He paused, then added with a jaunty twist, "Goldie."

Obviously bewildered and wary, she angled across the room to her own bed, her gaze never leaving him. "Don't try to con me, you gangster."

"I can't make any long-term promises, but you're safe for tonight."

"Hah." She pulled back a pile of thick, fluffy quilts. Her bedstead was tall and heavy; there were two mattresses and a set of springs topped by white sheets, several pillows, and the stack of quilts. The bed was wide enough for two, he decided. It had great pleasure potential, much like its owner.

She stripped her robe off and tossed it over the bed's tall corner post. The white linen gown floated around her, as revealing as a canvas tent but very graceful. She glanced over her shoulder as she climbed into bed, and saw him watching her.

"Get used to me," she said, frowning at him. Quickly she slid under the covers and pulled them to her waist as she lay down, her hair streaming across the pillows. The last rays of the banked fire cast amber light on her, along with seductive shadows.

Oh, I could easily get used to you, Douglas thought.

"Get used to *me*," he replied lightly. He pulled his sweater over his head and dropped it on the wooden table in the cell. Slowly he ran his hands over his bare chest and stomach. Even though he couldn't see her face well in the dim light, he felt sure that her eyes were on him. "Did you knit me any pajamas?" he asked. "Or maybe an electric blanket?"

"There's a set of long underwear in the bottom of the little chest of drawers."

"An appropriate place," he quipped, as he crossed the cell to the chest. The long johns were bright red. "Oh, good. Now I'll match my socks."

"I know you like to be well-dressed."

He tossed the long johns on the table and sat down in the wooden chair beside it. After he kicked his sandals off he unfastened his trousers. Then he stood to give Goldie the full effect. Slowly he pushed the trousers down his hips.

"You've got a nice private bathroom for changing clothes," she said quickly.

"You'll just have to put up with my lack of modesty. Don't watch, if it embarrasses you."

She mumbled something dire in Gaelic and ended with English. "I'm not embarrassed by the likes of you."

"Good." His trousers fell to his ankles. Across the room he heard an unmistakable gasp. Douglas glanced toward the chest of drawers. "Are there any shorts or briefs around here?" he asked innocently. "You'll have to forgive me for not asking before. I've been a little distracted."

"Aye, they're, uhmmm, somewhere." She cleared her throat. "The dresser. Second drawer from the bottom."

Douglas stepped out of his trousers and stretched

with as much show of nonchalance as he could muster, considering the state of his arousal. Wearing
nothing but knee-high red socks, he ambled across
to the chest and took his time finding a pair of
briefs.

Folding his naked body into the upholstered chair
near the bed, he drew one leg up, then the other.
With unhurried movements that would have done
justice to an exotic dancer, he teased the briefs along
his thighs, arching his back a little. His sense of
drama had won him A's in the college acting classes
he'd taken for fun.

Finally he stood, slid his hands over his rump,
tested the briefs' waistband, and gazed down at himself in solemn scrutiny. "Well, what do you think,
Goldie? Impressive, isn't it?"

From across the room came the deep, resonant
drone of snoring.

Douglas gazed at her dark form in disgruntled
surprise. It took him a second to realize that the
snoring was absurdly exaggerated.

He grinned. By the time he got into bed he was
laughing so hard that tears came to his eyes. He was
the prisoner of a woman who had infuriated, har-
rassed, and insulted him more than any person in
the world. He hated to admit it, but he was beginning to like her.

Four

> The mists of Talrigh still mourn,
> Haunted by spirits of Kincaid and MacRoth.
> Replayed eternally: Theft of the brooch,
> Clash of the steel,
> Spectral blood shed for honor of clans;
> War and wizardy—neither shall save them;
> Only true love shall soothe the pain and
> Heal wounds of the past,
> That ancient sorrows may sleep at last.

Elgiva read the old poem again, and frowned. *Only true love shall soothe the pain.* Her mother, solemn and practical, had always said that the line referred to love for Scotland. But her father, a daydreaming romantic, had insisted that it meant the love between a man and a woman. Considering their opposite natures, it was amazing that her parents had been so perfect together.

One Christmas night twenty-five years ago was etched indelibly in Elgiva's mind. She and Rob had tiptoed from bed, shivering, and had hidden behind the shabby drapes in the master hunt room at MacRoth Hall, giggling over the fact that both of their parents were tipsy from too much ale.

She and Rob had been entertained watching their

normally reserved mother and father snuggle close together on a sagging couch while a musty stag's head peered down at them with its one remaining glass eye. Rob had wrinkled his nose at the kissing and hugging, but Elgiva had been old enough to appreciate the romance of it.

Though it had hardly sounded like romance.

"David, you'll be a silly old man, the kind who sings to himself and dances under the full moon," Mother told Father between kisses.

Father laughed. "Aye, and I plan to live to be a thousand just to torment you."

"I'll scold you every day of it," she retorted, but nibbled his ear. Then she looked at him and said so low that Elgiva could barely hear, "When you pass on, I wish to follow the next second."

Mother had gotten that wish, though much sooner than a thousand years. Swallowing hard, Elgiva shut the book of poetry and sat gazing wistfully at the worn leather cover.

"That must be a cookbook. You look pensive—as if you've lost the recipe for something."

Douglas Kincaid's droll, richly timbered voice slipped into her veins like sweet wine. She looked up at him and blinked owlishly. He lounged in one corner of his cell, wearing nothing but his trousers. His torso glistened with sweat from all the push-ups he'd performed during the past two hours. The muscles of his chest and stomach trembled and flexed each time he inhaled.

"Lost the recipe," she repeated blankly.

Elgiva stared at the potent masculinity being displayed only a few meters away, behind thick bars. Who needed protecting from whom? She was beginning to resent those bars.

She had taken to reading the book of Scottish poetry to keep from ogling him helplessly. The sight of his hard, lean body pumping like an unstoppable machine had made her weak inside. Looking away hadn't solved the problem, because the soft, urgent sounds of his breathing had induced even more imaginings.

Now Elgiva leapt up and busied herself returning the book to a sideboard against one wall. "Lost a recipe. Aye, you might say that I did. Long ago. Well, time to go let Shom back in. If he stays out in the sunshine much longer, he'll have spring fever months before it's due."

Sensing Kincaid's dark eyes on her, Elgiva fussed with the other books stacked atop the table. "You've been in a bonnie mood today, Douglas. Things will go pleasantly if you keep your spirits up this way."

"I'm finally adjusting to life without phones, that's all. Do you want to know how many phone calls I average during a workday? Upward of a hundred. You did a cruel thing by making me give that up cold turkey. But if I'm mellowing out, it's only because I know that somebody's going to spring me from this joint soon."

"You'll be here until the MacRoth estate is free and clear. But if your fantasy cheers you, keep believing it. I like you when you're lighthearted."

"Why, *thank you.* I wouldn't want to depress you with my insignificant problems."

His taunt was mild—charming, in a sardonic way. She curtsied slightly, enjoying the new atmosphere. "Now if you'll excuse me, I've got to get my pudding started for supper."

He groaned. "You realize, of course, that I'm doing a push-up for every calorie you feed me."

"Then you should add a few thousand."

He shrugged, came forward, braced one long arm on the cell bars above his head, and leaned, hip-shot. He scanned her from head to foot, slowly. "Might as well do push-ups. I've got no other way to release my tension."

"Poor man." She sighed dramatically and added, as if speaking to a third party, "And him so accustomed to getting his way with women." She eyed him boldly. "You won't find a good wife if you wait much longer. You're getting a wee bit long in the tooth."

He smiled wickedly. "It's not the length of my tooth that matters to women. Don't worry about me, doll. I'll marry the *perfect* wife."

"Oh? Dumb as an ox and twice as forgiving?"

"No. She'll be extremely intelligent and have a brilliant grasp of business. I want a partner—someone I can trust to head a few of my biggest projects. But she'll also be an expert at entertaining. She'll be the kind of woman who can organize a party for fifty of my favorite stockbrokers one night and host the President and First Lady for lunch the next day. She'll know how to pick the classiest clothes and the best wine."

"I think you need a harem. The poor woman is going to be worked to death."

"Oh, she'll be a brilliant manager, and her staff will handle the details. Whenever she needs a rest, I'll take her down to my island in the Caribbean. Or to the chateau outside Paris. Or the ranch in Colorado. Or the estate in Florida. Or my *new* estate in Scotland—"

"Don't marry a homebody. She'd get confused trying to figure out which home."

"I'll want her to love kids and dogs."

"Well, you can always buy her a few."

"She'll be beautiful, of course."

"Of course."

"And blond. And blue-eyed."

"And petite. You forgot petite."

He sighed happily, as if picturing the future Mrs. Kincaid. "Yes, petite. Thank you for reminding me."

"But you'd be mean to marry a petite woman, Douglas. She'd only get crushed by your ego. A flattened blue-eyed blonde. Ugh. You need a big, swarthy woman who'll remind you of your Neanderthal background."

"Doll, I've got one of the world's best collections of sapphires. I've been buying them for years. They're the perfect color for a blue-eyed blonde to wear. Now what would I do with ten million dollars worth of sapphires if I changed my mind?"

"You don't want me to tell you what you should do with your sapphires."

He chuckled sardonically. "No, I think I can guess." Arching a black brow, he gave her an appraising look. "So why haven't you remarried?"

"There aren't a lot of likely men in Druradeen. It's a small place."

"What? You don't know any eligible bachelors in the kidnapping business?"

Elgiva huffed in exasperation. "Plus I have no dowry to offer." She shot him a scathing look. "Yet."

"Dream on, doll." He studied her, looking intrigued. "Why do you need a dowry?"

"Marriages are built on practical concerns. Land, money, children. I have naught to offer."

His gaze trailed down her sweater and skirt. "Oh, I wouldn't say that. In that green evening gown you could have made any man forget about dirt, dough, and dynasties." His voice became coy. "In the meantime, I wouldn't mind being entertained. Have you got the green dress here? Wear that when you do your knitting."

"It's a joy to watch such an overindulged beast learn the merits of patience."

"Patience? You mean I'll get what I want, eventually?"

Elgiva winced inwardly. Why was her mouth making offers that her honor couldn't keep? "You can't *always* get what you want, Douglas. Perhaps this time you'll get what you *need,* instead."

He looked amused. "Did you ever write a song for the Rolling Stones?"

"Hmmmph. A rock and roll group. Mick Jagger. I know them. Their albums are sold in the stores in Edinburgh."

"You didn't pull off a kidnapping in the middle of

Manhattan without knowing the city pretty well. How much time have you spent in the United States?"

"You won't get incriminating information out of me. But that was a nice try."

He slid a hand down his sweaty stomach, stroking the streak of silver hair amidst the black as he gazed thoughtfully at her. His hand moved with the unselfconscious sensuality of a man who was very comfortable with his body. Elgiva tracked the up-and-down action without blinking.

"I'll get a lot out of you before I'm done," he murmured, with a thin, confident smile.

She exhaled raggedly and clucked her tongue. "If you can catch me, you can have me."

"I'll consider that a promise."

"Hoots, man! You'd wish that you'd been tossed into a pit with a dozen lions, instead."

"You're always so creative with your threats. What do you do when you're not ·kidnapping people? I know! You're a tax collector."

She waved toward the other room, with its kitchen. "Perhaps I'm a chef." Elgiva pointed to the pile of knitting she kept in a woven basket. "Perhaps I make sweaters for a living." She gestured at the books. "I could be a teacher. Or a writer."

"No. Hmmm, let me guess." He hooked his thumb into his trousers and let his fingers tap lightly on the dark woolen material not far above the bulge in the crotch. Elgiva's stomach quivered. Was his enticement calculated, or was it enticement at all? Perhaps she only imagined it. Overwrought fantasies were the price one paid for years of emptiness.

"You rob banks," he said, studying her through narrowed eyes. "Because God knows there's not any other way to make a lot of money around Druradeen. You needed quite a bit to fund your little kidnapping project. Of course, the other fanatics in your gang contributed some dough too."

"My *gang*? Next you'll be calling me 'Ma MacBarker.'

I keep telling you that there's no gang, Douglas. I sold some jewelry of my mother's to pay my kidnapping expenses."

"Another thing. Could you please pronounce my name correctly? It's *Dug-less.*"

"Not in the homeland. You're a *Dooglas* here." She took a deep breath and plunged forward, hoping that his mood would make him receptive, finally. "You're Dooglas Kincaid, the last of the Kincaids of Talrigh, one of the mightiest clans of the highlands."

He gazed at her silently, looking bewildered and a little angry. "You said something about my clan once before. 'Kincaid' may be a Scottish surname, but it's not traceable. I've paid experts to try."

"You didn't have to *pay.* All you had to do was come to the right people yourself. We don't take to foreigners sending their stooges to do a Scot's duty for him."

He straightened ominously. "Are you trying to make me feel some kind of old-world kinship? You think I'd fall for that kind of hoax?" His next few words were pithy and obscene.

Elgiva rebuked herself for telling him. He wasn't ready to believe. "I'm not making it up, Douglas. I'm not trying to win your friendship with a lie."

"Right. I'm gonna believe *that* too." His eyes flickered with disgust. "If I were of Scottish descent, my people would have discovered it."

"Only if you were of any clan other than the Kincaids. There's not much history written on them, you see. Most of what is known are stories passed down among the other clans. Only a few ballads and poems mention the Kincaids. No more than that."

"I am *not* of Scottish descent!" He jabbed a finger through the bars at her. "Nobody knows how the first Kincaid got to America, or why, or when. Don't try any sentimental crap on me, doll!"

Elgiva drew her chin up and eyed him coldly. "The crown banished Tammas Kincaid and sentenced him to live the rest of his life in the American colonies. The year was 1722. Tammas's clan had been destroyed on the crown's orders, and all mention of their history taken from the records. Even their ancient clan charter was revoked. The Kincaids were no more—it was as if they had never existed." She put her hands on her hips. "And *that*, Douglas, is how your ancestor ended up in America."

"You could have concocted a more sympathetic story if you wanted to stir up my interest."

"Aye, I could have made up all sorts of charming tales about the Kincaids. But I didn't do it. I told you the unadorned truth." She held out her hands in supplication. "But your people *do* have a proud history. Even their destruction was glorious. And if you'll just listen—"

"Here it comes," he said sarcastically. "The hook. Forget it, doll. Save your legends to peddle to the tourists. After you get out of prison, of course. Ye Old Legend Teller. I'll give you a booth."

She balled her hands into fists. "Why do you want to ruin something without at least trying to understand it first?"

"I'm not going to ruin anything! When Douglas Kincaid does something, he does it first-class! The best gardeners, the best decorators, the best management. I'll turn the MacRoth estate into a showplace."

"You'll just be a foreign *laird* despised by all the dear people you evict from their lands and their homes only so that you can have privacy."

"They can move to another estate and pay rent there! Haven't you ever heard of *moving*? Is that a totally unknown concept in your country?"

"They've lived in and around Druradeen for generations!" She threw up her hands in despair. "You're a fool! You'll come to the same end as the rest of your kin, with your pride in shambles!"

"My *kin* are in America, where their pride is very healthy, thank you."

"Och! I'd like as not get more sense out of a stone wall!"

Elgiva wheeled and marched to the other room, then slammed the door behind her. Angrily she shoved pots and pans around on the stove. Forget the pudding, she told herself. She'd fry some lamb chops to a black crisp and then set them outdoors to get cold and hard. Let his pride gnaw on those!

She lit a burner, flung a heavy skillet onto the stove top next to it, then dug her fingers into a container of sausage drippings and threw the gooey oil at the skillet. It missed and hit the burner.

Elgiva jumped back immediately as flames shot up, but they caught her outstretched hand and ignited the grease on her fingertips. Like some horrible magic trick, flames sprouted there. She stabbed her hand into her skirt and suffocated the flames in its plaid folds. A wave of pain radiated up her arm. Her stomach twisted sickly, and her legs almost collapsed.

She smothered the stove fire with the skillet and cut the burner off. Staggering, she went to the sink and ran water over her fingers. Their ends were an ugly red, and the tips of the nails looked as if they'd melted. Elgiva nearly gagged on the pungent odor.

The pain made her shiver and chew her lip, but after a few minutes the icy water revived her. Breathing heavily, she wrapped her hand in a towel and returned to the main room, where she kept a medicine chest under her bed.

Douglas Kincaid stepped out of his washroom, dressed in the thick blue robe she'd provided. He had just taken a shower, and was toweling his wet hair vigorously. When he saw her heading for the bed he grunted. "Need a nap? You must be worn out from carrying that self-righteous attitude around."

Elgiva ignored him and sank to her knees. With her good hand she dragged a heavy wooden chest from beneath the bed and flipped the lid open. As she fished through tubes and bottles and medical implements, she heard Kincaid moving to the front of his cell. "Is that your witch's kit?" he taunted. "Gonna mix a little 'eye of MacNewt' into the pudding? Or maybe some hemlock?"

Nausea assailed her again. She leaned against the bedstead and shut her eyes, waiting for it to pass. Across the room Kincaid grew very still; either that or she couldn't hear his movements above the buzzing in her ears. Finally the buzzing faded. Elgiva realized that Kincaid was speaking to her.

"Just bring the chest and come here," he repeated. "Let me help, if I can." Amazingly, he sounded serious and reassuring, almost gentle.

Elgiva wiped cold perspiration from her forehead and looked at him, her head still resting on the side of the mattress. "Why?"

One corner of his mouth quirked up in a grim smile. "Because I'll starve if you faint."

"Don't worry, Douglas. I'll have a go at cooking as soon as I get myself fixed up."

"What happened to you?"

She lifted her wrapped hand, trying not to wince, then let it rest in her lap again. "I burned my fingers in some grease. That's what I get for letting a Kincaid make me mad and reckless."

"Come here. Just come here and sit at the table. Let me see what I can do for your toasted claws."

Her head muddled by the pain, she ignored the warning that said Douglas Kincaid was probably going to do something awful to her. Elgiva got up, wavered a moment, then took a deep breath and clasped the chest's handle. She pulled the awkward box across the room to the serving table and hoisted it to the top. Then she slumped into a chair and put her head down weakly. She eased her burned hand toward the opening in the cell bars.

Kincaid tucked his robe a little tighter around himself and put a chair close to his side of the bars.

He sat down and reached through with both hands, his gaze locked on her. "I've seen mimes who weren't as white-faced as you are right now."

"The burns aren't so bad," she told him, panting lightly. Elgiva raised her head and looked at him stoically. "It's just the idea of them. Of being burned in a fire. My parents died that way."

He took her hand between his, and she waited fearfully to see how her trust would be rewarded. But he was very careful not to hurt her as he unwrapped the towel, and when her hand lay bare in his he held it with supreme gentleness. Confused, she warned him softly, "I can't turn you loose, no matter how much you surprise me."

He opened the medicine chest and studied the contents as if he hadn't heard her. "My sister was burned badly once. When she was six or seven. We had a crummy apartment that was impossible to keep heated in the winter—it had old steam radiators. One developed a crack. She didn't hear it hissing, and she stood too close. It gave her a second-degree burn across the middle of her back. For six weeks everybody in the family took turns changing the dressings. It hurt her so much that she and I always ended up crying."

"But how did she miss hearing the steam?"

He lifted a tube of ointment from the chest and studied the label. "Will this do?"

"Aye."

Kincaid opened the tube with the fingers of one hand, while the other hand continued to hold hers. "She's deaf. She had a severe infection when she was a baby, and it ruined her hearing."

"I'm sorry." Elgiva marveled at his dexterity as he manipulated the ointment onto her fingers with a featherlight touch. Those brawny hands were very good at small, human things. She pictured Kincaid as she had never imagined him before—a worried, upset teenager gently putting medicine on his little sister's back.

"She's been a great success as a model despite her deafness though," Elgiva ventured, anxious to know more. "I read about her. Putting her beautiful hands and feet in all those ads. 'The Queen of Spare Parts,' someone called her."

"You studied my family?"

"Aye. I know that you bought your mother a mansion in Chicago and that her hobby is managing middleweight boxers. I know that your brother is a professor of archaeology."

He chuckled. "You were thorough. Why was my family important?"

"To learn what you hold dear."

Suddenly his hand tightened around hers, the grip almost, but not quite, hurting her scalded fingers. His gaze bored into her. "Is my family in any danger?"

"No! I swear it!" Elgiva looked at him with such horror that he eased his hold. "And neither are you! I swear it, Douglas!"

"You have to admit, kidnapping my family would give you more leverage."

"Aye, but one Kincaid is all I can handle. Besides, it wouldn't be fair to terrify innocent people."

"Oh, but it's *fine* to terrify a criminal like me, huh?"

"You don't look terrified."

"So what did you conclude from studying my family?"

"That you have your ancestors' deep need for kinship. A good sign."

"Dammit, don't start with the history lecture again. That's a hopeless ruse, Goldie." He finished dabbing ointment on her fingertips. His voice became quaint. "Little girls who make up fairy tales are likely to get burned by their lies."

"It was pork grease that did the burning. My lies are not nearly so painful. And I *am* telling the truth about your Scottish—"

"I said stop it." The expression on his face conveyed fierce and unyielding stubbornness. "If you want this prisoner to stay on good behavior, don't ever try to pull that Kincaid clan hoax again."

"Then don't ever talk about your plans for the MacRoth estate. If you try, I'll open the windows and the door and turn off the heat and let you sit and shiver!"

"It's a deal."

Elgiva bit her lip and looked at him anxiously. So much for those topics of conversation. She'd have to use a difference tactic to coax him.

She lowered her gaze humbly and said in a low, apologetic tone, "I don't want you to be angry with me anymore. It's sad that we could have been such grand friends aside from all this trouble. I truly regret what I've taken from us."

To her chagrin, he sat back, held his stomach, and let deep shouts of laughter roll out of his throat. Elgiva bristled.

When he finally got himself under control again, he wiped his eyes and studied her merrily. "Damn. What a performance. You belong on a soap opera. *As the Worm Turns.*"

Abashed, she looked away and grumbled half-heartedly, "Even if we canna trust each other, can we find some neutral ground and exist in peace?"

"Until I'm rescued," he countered.

"Until I set you loose," she corrected.

He took her injured hand again. "All right. It's a deal. Want to shake on it?"

Elgiva eyed him with mock disgust. "Want to wear your nose a little more to the left?"

"Nope. Let's make peace."

"Peace, then."

With that truce a Kincaid and a MacRoth did something that broke seven hundred years of tradition. They began to enjoy each other's company.

•   •   •

Elgiva stood on a grassy knoll, one hand resting on a cairn that was as old as Scotland. It was, in effect, a war memorial. Knights had ridden past it on their way to battle, each taking a rock to toss away on the journey. Each of those who returned placed a new rock on the cairn in gratitude.

The era of knights had faded; the ritual had not. Whether on their way to fight a rival clan or riding against the English, the highland warriors took and replaced the stones. Elgiva had removed one before the trip to America.

Her battle was far from over. She watched the gloomy winter skies impatiently. In the distance she finally saw two men crest a ridge. She rushed forward eagerly. When she reached them, she hugged Rob and nodded to Duncan.

Rob had reverted to his favorite clothes—black trousers and a bright yellow sweater. A large wool drape in the yellow-and-black tartan of the MacRoths was held by brass pins at his shoulders. The ends hung down both sides of his body, swaying against his thighs in the gusty breeze. Pulled at an angle over his chestnut hair was a yellow tam. Duncan, who stood beside him grimacing in the wind, looked gray and dull by comparison.

"How's the devil Kincaid today?" Rob asked.

"Still as happy as when I radioed you two nights ago. He's never stopped expecting to be rescued at any minute, but he's not chomping at the bit anymore. He and I have been playing card games and chess—oh, he's a competitive beast, but so am I! And he's told me all about his family—"

"Is he your prisoner or your guest for tea?" Duncan demanded loudly. "I don't approve of this fraternization."

Even Rob frowned a little at her enthusiasm. "You're not getting fond of the man, are you, Ellie?"

The pang of guilt she felt was submerged in a wave of indignation. "If the man comes to like me, wouldn't that serve our goal? I'm just trying to win his change of heart so that he'll no' regret it so much when he loses his land deal. After all, I'm the one who has a lifetime of jeopardy ahead of me if he won't forgive and forget!"

"Douglas Kincaid doesn't forgive and forget," Duncan said sourly. "That's why you're wasting your time trying to turn him into a pet. You should be teaching him to fear you; not to kiss your hand."

Rob looked at their kinsman with barely leashed disgust. "My sister knows her plan, Duncan. We'd best leave her to it."

"Aye," Elgiva said proudly. "We're in no danger of losing our catch—"

"I was about to tell you, Ellie"—Rob's eyes darkened—"some high-priced investigator is working on Kincaid's case. A man named Audubon."

"He came to the village asking for you and Rob," Duncan interjected. "I put him off, but he's suspicious. Rob's hiding out in the old Lockhart cottage, to be on the safe side. This Audubon has figured something out, though he doesn't know specifics yet."

No news could have alarmed her more. Elgiva realized that her hands had risen to her throat in a gesture of self-defense. Slowly she forced them down to her sides. "He may find me, but he won't connect anyone else to the kidnapping. No matter what he suspects. And that's as we planned it."

"He's not just some hired lackey of Kincaid's," Duncan told her. "They're old friends. They were soldiers together in the Vietnamese War. Kincaid saved his life. In fact, that's how Kincaid got that little scar on his face. He was hit by shrapnel carrying the man to safety. This Audubon has a debt of honor to repay."

Elgiva shut her eyes and groaned with dismay. Even so, a small part of her noted that Douglas's scar had been won through bravery, and she was glad. She looked at Rob and Duncan worriedly.

"There's naught we can do to protect ourselves that we haven't already done. Just let me know if you hear any news."

"Aye. Be sure to call in at your regular times."

Elgiva nodded. "I'll be heading back now."

From his back Rob took a knapsack stuffed with supplies. As he helped her slip it over her shoulders he asked, "By the by, does the great Kincaid live like a pig without all his valets and maids to look after him?"

Elgiva laughed. "Oh, no. He's very neat. When he washes his underwear, he hangs it out on the cell bars in neat little rows, briefs all evenly spaced, all turned with the crotches in the same direction—" She stopped when she saw Rob staring at her in shock.

"The bastard puts his personal items out where you can see them? Even Jonathan wouldn't have done that, and he was your husband. Are you giving Kincaid liberties that would shame Jonathan's memory?"

Elgiva's anger flared. She had been a good wife, and everyone knew it. "Let's not talk about Jonathan. I won't have you lecture me, Robbie MacRoth. You've no call to. Nor have you any understanding of what it means to marry at a young, ignorant age."

"Just because Mother passed on before she could arrange my marriage banns—"

"You've had a freedom of choice I never knew!"

"Ellie, you never complained about it before."

"I'm not complaining now. But don't lecture me about Douglas."

"*Douglas*, is it?" Duncan yelped. "I hope you're not calling the reiver by his personal name."

"Aye, and he calls me Goldie," Elgiva snapped. She glared at both men with equal rebuke. "And when the moon is full, I take him out to meet the Elf Queen and we dance together in the glens!"

She blew Rob an angry kiss and marched away,

her defenses raised so high that she couldn't see the folly of her own protests.

Douglas was in great danger of declaring that he didn't want Goldie to step into the next room, much less leave him alone for her long daily walks. He tried to tell himself that he was simply so damned bored that anyone's company would have been precious.

But he wasn't the kind of person who needed a lot of company. One didn't get to the top of a business empire by seeking out other people, but rather by making them seek *him*. With Goldie he woke up in the middle of the night only to watch her sleep. She was definitely special.

Now he lay on his stomach, his chin propped on a pillow at the foot of the bed, one long arm hanging off the side. Sam lay just beyond the bars, muzzle on paws. Sam made groaning sounds from time to time. Not only was he stuffed to the jowls from a lunch of roast mutton and butter cake, he was disgruntled because for once Goldie had left him behind.

Douglas idly withdrew his leather sandal from under the bed. He tossed it outside the cell. It fell in the far corner beyond the fireplace. He waved toward it. "Fetch, Sam."

Sam lumbered to his feet, yawning, retrieved the sandal, then dropped it just inside the bars. He sat down and looked at his master as if waiting for more.

An idea came to Douglas. He got up and glanced around the cottage, then pointed to a neat little bundle of clothes on the foot of Goldie's bed. "Fetch."

Sam brought the bundle back. Douglas untied a soft cotton undershirt. Inside was an array of sweet-smelling clothes, freshly washed and dried. He lifted a bra made of nothing more than sheer white lace. The mental image of Goldie's firm, abundant flesh peeking through that lace made him shut his eyes and indulge in a lusty daydream.

The daydream was suffused with a tenderness that quieted him. As much as anything he wanted to hear her whisper his name, and he wanted to see her amber eyes light up with trust.

Sam woofed impatiently, breaking the spell. Douglas put the bra aside and picked up a pair of mittens. A label was sewn inside the cuff of one. He whistled in surprise. *Woolens by Elgiva MacRoth, Druradeen, Terkleshire.*

Elgiva. He said the lyrical name over and over, thinking that it suited her beautifully, being so Gaelic and so old-fashioned. Elgiva MacRoth. What had her married name been? Why didn't she use it?

He ran his fingertips over the mittens, marveling at the workmanship. Elgiva MacRoth, a weaver. It made perfect sense. Weaver of fairy tales. Weaver of enchantments. Feeling as if he'd learned a great deal more than her name, he put the mittens back in the bundle and set it aside. He pointed toward the sideboard across from the bed. "Fetch."

Sam had more choices this time, because the sideboard contained a variety of objects. He came back carrying a small bound book with gilt edges. Douglas opened it and stared in amazement. It was a diary of sorts. It started on the day of his kidnapping. The notes were cryptic, but he absorbed them with fascination, and certain ones he read many times.

Flight home—Kincaid slept soundly. D. threatened to hit him, just for spite. Such a bully! R. and I wouldn't permit it. To watch D. strike a strong man such as Kincaid when he was helpless was more than I could bear.

First night—He sleeps in his clothes, exhausted and angry. I stand here shivering in the darkness and watch him, thinking that I have never felt so much desire in my whole life. What would twelve years of marriage have been like with Kincaid? I wish I could miss Jonathan. I wish I could remember the last time he touched me— was it six months before he died, or more? I cannot watch Kincaid this way. It is disastrous.

First smile—Kincaid showed his teeth, and for once, he wasn't snarling at me! What a dangerous, glorious-looking man!

Jolting Jack—Tonight he told me about his father, who was paralyzed from an injury he received during a boxing match. Kincaid was only five years old when it happened. Criminal element—"strong-armed" J. Jack to "set-up" a match, then "double-crossed" him. Suffered for years before he died. It hurts Kincaid even now. Can see it in his eyes. Can't tell him about my parents and the fire at MacRoth Hall—too much revealing background information. But I'm sure he'd sympathize. Kincaid has a very deep heart. If only he would open it to me.

Slowly Douglas shut the book. His fingers played over it, stroking. The warmth and confusion inside him was a torment. He was not accustomed to being any kind of prisoner, and now he was trapped not only by bars but also by warring emotions.

And if Elgiva MacRoth ever learned that he'd read her diary, *war* would be a mild description for what she'd wage in revenge. Carrying both her clothes and the diary, Douglas rose and went to the cell bars. He couldn't aim well enough to make certain that he'd toss the diary back atop the sideboard.

So he did the next best thing—with a graceful underhand swing he popped the diary onto her bed, then followed with the bundle of clothes. Maybe she'd think that brownies had been at work.

Sam galloped over to retrieve everything again. "No!" Douglas called. The dog halted near the bed and looked at Douglas curiously, awaiting new orders. On a whim Douglas gestured toward the open door to the front room. "Fetch!"

Sam disappeared into the room. Douglas heard rustling and bumping noises. Then Sam came back, his tail wagging proudly. He trotted straight to the cell and deposited his gift into Douglas's outstretched hand. Its long cord trailed onto the floor.

"Well, well, well, she kept this a secret," Douglas said happily. He lay down again and, smiling with anticipation, tucked the radio microphone under his pillow. He had a hostage of his own now, and she would have to pay dearly to get it back.

Five

Elgiva and Rob had agreed upon a routine. She would radio him three times a week between midnight and half past. If she failed to call, he would show up at the cottage within an hour.

Two days after their rendezvous at the cairn she sat down at a small table in the front room and flipped a switch on her radio unit. Then she reached for the mike.

After a stunned moment, she rose and peered behind the radio. No mike. She scanned the tabletop as if the mike could hide in plain sight. She searched the wooden floor under the table. Growing frantic, she searched the whole room—under the stove and sink, inside the shower stall, even on the storage shelves along the walls.

The mike *had* to be in the room. Elgiva muttered out loud, "All right, my playful brownies, I *know* you've been at work here, just as I know I didn't leave my diary laying atop my bed the other day." She blanched as the twin mysteries of the displaced diary and the missing microphone connected themselves to an answer. Douglas! But how? *Fetch, Sam.*

Furious, Elgiva slung open the door to the main room and strode across to his cell, her robe flapping on either side like the wings of an angry terry cloth bird. The room was dark except for the small electric lantern on Douglas's table. He sat in a dramatic pool of light, putting his bold, beautiful script on sheets of notebook paper she'd given him. He had asked her to send management notes—anonymously, of course—to his assistant in New York.

Elgiva had no intention of doing anything so foolish, but she'd said that she'd think about it, just to make him happy. She had been doing a lot of things lately just to make him happy.

"Where is it, you thieving snake?" Elgiva demanded. She grabbed his cell bars and glared in at him. "I thought we had a truce!"

He looked up calmly, stroked a hand down the front of his white sweater—a sweater she'd made with her own two hands, damn him!—and inquired innocently, "May I help you?"

"Give me the microphone back! It won't do you any good to keep it!"

"Oh, *that*. No use for me to keep it, you say? But if I keep it, won't your pals come running to see why Goldie has stopped calling? I'd really like to meet your friends."

"There's no one to meet!"

"You're getting fresh food from somewhere, and I doubt we're within walking distance to Ye Old Highland Supermarket."

"All right. I have deliveries made, but the delivery people don't know I'm a kidnapper."

"Could I get a pizza, then? Or maybe some Chinese food? A little MacMoo Goo Gai Pan?"

"You won't get anything but trouble unless you give the mike back! I'll let you starve!"

"Go ahead. I've developed enough fat to hibernate if I have to." He slapped his stomach, which despite his words looked as flat as ever, thanks to the hours of exercise he performed every day.

Elgiva took several calming breaths then said in a patient voice, "Douglas, you won't get anywhere with this trick. You'll accomplish naught."

"Hmmm." He rose and went to his bed, where he retrieved the mike from under a pillow. "All right. I'll make you a trade. For the past ten days I've suffered agonies"—he clasped his chest with one hand—"because I've been deprived of what I live for."

"A man can live without custom-made underwear," she retorted. "Trust me."

"My deals! My excitement! The thrill of negotiating! I'll wither and die unless you give me an occasional dose of power!"

"What would you be wanting?"

He met her eyes with a gaze that had suddenly become very intense. "Five minutes."

Elgiva felt her pulse thumping hard in her throat. "Of what?"

"Of you."

She took a step back, her mouth open in shock. "Doing what?"

"Just standing still. And not making any protests."

"Standing where?"

He rested one large, sinewy hand palm up on a crossbar. Slowly his index finger beckoned her. "Right here." When she gazed at him in speechless disbelief, he clucked his tongue as if she were being silly. "It won't hurt. In fact, you may not want to leave when five minutes are up."

Elgiva understood perfectly now, and her knees went weak. A traitorous little voice cheered in the back of her mind. The combination of anger and excitement made her feel too warm inside her robe and gown.

"I'll just let you starve," she whispered.

"No, you won't do that." His voice was low, throaty. "And I won't do anything terrible to you. I think you know that."

"Give me the microphone, Douglas. I mean, *Dugless.* See? I can say your name the way you want. I can make compromises. I can—"

"Five minutes. Or no mike."

Elgiva shivered with defeat. "F—five minutes. Swear it," she ordered.

He made an X on his chest. "Cross my heart and hope a conglomerate of Japanese businessmen launches a hostile takeover of Kincaid Hotels Worldwide if I'm telling a lie." He laid the mike on his table, then fiddled with a setting on his wristwatch. "In five minutes we'll hear the opening notes of Bobbie Royal's 'Blues for the Night.' Then I'll give the mike back. Ready?"

She passed a hand over her forehead. "No. But go to it, you lecherous monster."

"How romantic!" He snapped his fingers and pointed to the bars. "Right there. As close as you can get. Hands on the crossbar." When she complied he nodded with satisfaction. Then he stepped up to the bars, and abruptly his face was only a hand's width from hers. The heat and fresh, soapy fragrance of his body radiated over her; his breath, scented with the smoky richness of the Scotch he'd drunk after supper, brushed across her cheeks.

"Set?" he asked softly. She could barely think, much less speak. She nodded. He lifted his wrist and touched a tiny button. "Go."

His hand slipped between the bars and slid under her loose hair. Slowly he cupped the back of her head. "Tilt your face up a little," he murmured. "And put it between the bars, please."

Quivering, Elgiva did. Her heart raced madly as he angled his head and lowered his mouth on hers with incredible patience. Languid eternities passed before his firm, nuzzling lips settled fully on hers.

He nudged and tugged at her mouth, using an endless variety of skillful little movements until she found herself giving them in return. She was moving her lips against his, helplessly enjoying herself. Breaking contact just enough to speak, he whispered, "Open your mouth, please."

Elgiva moaned softly and told herself that she had no choice. His eyes, heavy lidded with desire, studied her parted lips with obvious approval before he kissed her again. This time he slid his tongue inside her mouth, and she sagged against the bars, clutching them for support.

Jonathan had never kissed her like this. For years she'd imagined what it would feel like to have a man share this intimacy, but what Douglas Kincaid was doing frightened her with its intensity.

He was dissolving her reason and resistance, making her think that she'd do anything for him, give him anything he wanted as long as he satisfied the sublime torment she'd suffered for days. She couldn't stop kissing him, and when he made low, gruff sounds of encouragement, she frantically began exploring his mouth as he was exploring hers.

The breath crashed in her lungs when both of his hands went to the front of her nightgown. His fingers dug between the buttons. He moved his lips away from hers and dropped kisses on her eyes and cheeks. In between he asked hoarsely, "How many nightgowns do you have?"

Elgiva's concentration centered on pressing her lips to his throat. "Two, I think," she murmured in a daze of sensation.

He chuckled, the sound strained. "Good. I don't want you to do without later."

With only that warning he ripped the gown down the center. Elgiva cried out in shock, but an even wilder excitement flared in her blood. He sensed it, because his hands went quickly to her exposed breasts and grasped them with calculated roughness, his thumbs scrubbing the nipples.

Elgiva sought his mouth again and clung to its fierce, promising focus. She realized dimly that she was whimpering and squirming, and that his hands were trembling as they moved over her, stroking her neck and shoulders, then her breasts again, then moving down the shivering skin of her stomach.

Suddenly he grasped her waist, arching her slightly and bringing the feverish skin of her breasts and belly against the cool, sleek bars. Elgiva was trapped and could only protest with a rough moan when he deserted her mouth. Then she gasped with elation as his lips moved down her neck and chest.

No fierce highland gale was ever more dangerous than the sensations that swept over her when he tantalized her breasts with the careful savagery of his teeth and the tug of his lips. Elgiva wrapped her hands around the cell bars and rested her face against the unyielding barrier; she wanted to tear it down.

Incredibly, there was more. His breath hot and ragged against her skin, Douglas trailed kisses down her stomach. By the time she realized what he intended to do, he was kneeling in front of her, his mouth hurried and uninhibited. His hands slid behind her hips and tilted her forward. Quickly he found her sweetest ache. Elgiva whispered his name in disbelief.

What he was doing was not something two people in their circumstances should share so easily, so naturally. But when pleasure shimmered through her like heat waves, she lost control. She felt as if she were vibrating between his harshly gripping hands and his boldly giving mouth. Every emotion they had shared in the past ten days exploded in that moment.

She was the ocean crashing against the craggy Scottish coast, compelled to surge forward again and again, bursting against a force as strong as her own. Elgiva sank against the bars, and his hold on her was the only reason she didn't fall.

Slowly he let her slide down, his lips moving upwards in a sensuous reversal of their earlier path. He bit her stomach gently, licked the valley between her breasts, then made a sound of surrender and sank his mouth onto her nipples. She settled in a limp heap in front of him, her damp hair cascading around her face, her body and emotions drained of resistance.

He slid his hands under the curtain of hair and

cupped her face. When he turned it to his gaze, she opened her eyes groggily and whimpered at the desire in his expression. Surely there was affection there too. She couldn't let herself think otherwise.

His knees were spread wide on the floor—his posture was the crouch of a man filled with desperately restrained energy and frustration. His chest moved with shallow, fast breaths. "Open the cell door," he told her in a hoarse whisper. "I'll come out or you come in. I don't care about escaping. I just don't want these bars between us."

Elgiva looked at him numbly as bleak regret filled her chest. She'd never know if he'd seduced her simply to win his freedom. It didn't really matter. She couldn't betray her family and neighbors.

An even more painful thought tore at her—she wanted to share everything in her life with this man. She wanted to share everything in his life. But that was impossible. With a tormented cry Elgiva pulled away from him and buried her face in her hands.

Tense silence stretched between them. She heard him struggling for composure, then cursing softly— sadly?—under each quick breath. Other sounds told her that he was standing and moving about.

Elgiva raised her head as he knelt beside her again. She gazed without victory at the microphone he placed on the floor beside her. With all the irony its expensive little soul could muster, his watch blurted the opening notes from "Blues in the Night."

Five minutes. The tenor of her life had been changed totally, all in less than five minutes. She put a shaking hand on the microphone and pulled it into her lap. "Thank you," she murmured. Considering what he'd just done to her, the words were both a lie and a vastly inadequate show of gratitude.

"The world is full of rewards, Goldie," he told her gruffly. "You deserve all of them." He reached through the bars and stroked her hair. "You could be so happy with me. Let's get out of here, Goldie. Forget about everything else. Let me take you places you've never been before."

"You already have," she said, her voice breaking. "But I can't stay. I must go back to the real world now. I'm sorry."

"Don't go—" he called, but she was already on her feet and moving swiftly toward the other room.

Once there she shut the door and blocked it with her body as if he might find a way through. Crying, Elgiva looked down at her torn gown and flushed skin. If he hadn't already.

Elgiva barely spoke to Douglas for the next three days, and he was supremely glad. The incident between them had torn his convictions apart. How could he hurt this woman or anything she loved? It made him furious to be at the mercy of self-doubt. The MacRoth project was good, damned good, for both the people and the preservation of their heritage.

As soon as his people had shown him pictures of the MacRoth land and the grand old manor house, he'd been enthralled. Nowhere had looked more like home to him. He was determined to add the place to his collection. He wasn't going to rip apart their ancient forests or plant hotels on the majestic green hills. The land's untouched atmosphere was its appeal—he'd keep most of it for himself and turn the town into a resort.

He didn't even care whether he made a profit on the deal. It was the challenge he needed so badly; anything to relieve the boredom and discontent that had begun to plague him in the past year.

All he'd ever wanted was to be somebody. In his late teens he'd thought that he'd make his name as a boxer, the way his father had tried to do. But the army had set him back a couple of years, and afterward his mother, who knew boxing better than most of the professional managers in the sport, had told him frankly that he wasn't good enough to be a champion, and he had trusted her opinion.

Business was his arena. There he had proved to be one of the best in the world. For years that had been enough—one deal after another, millions piling on top of millions, luxury atop luxury. He'd thought that he'd never get tired of it.

But he had. And it frightened him. What else was there to accomplish? He'd donated millions to charity; he had loaned his name and connections to dozens of good causes; he'd built youth clubs in ghettos and funded clinics in third-world countries. Of course, there was still plenty of that kind of work to do, but he had a whole staff of people to handle it. It wasn't anything but another Kincaid project to him. Supporting causes had become just another form of entertainment, and he felt guilty because he looked on it that way.

Now he felt fresh and intrigued, and because he was blunt about his own emotions he admitted that Elgiva MacRoth was the reason. He needed this project; he needed her even more. What he had to do was get control of the situation and then prove that his plan was the best thing for her.

When she went for her daily walk, Douglas paced his cell and looked at his freshly washed long johns he'd hung out to dry on a chair, the arms and legs arranged to dry without wrinkles. A neat row of white briefs decorated the cell bars, while a precision line of socks marched along the edge of his table. Mama Kincaid had given her three children a strict sense of discipline about their habits and their goals. She'd be pleased to see that years of maid service hadn't dimmed her efforts.

Douglas sat down on his bed and chuckled ruefully. If he wanted to control Elgiva as much as she controlled him, he would have to change his tactics. He stared at his wash day display in amused disgust. The only thing he had under control right now was his underwear.

• • •

A week after the shattering episode involving the microphone, Elgiva faced her brother and Duncan at their usual rendezvous point and boldly asserted that Douglas Kincaid was a fair man who might offer compromises if she released him.

Rob listened in grim silence as she described how pleasant and reflective Kincaid had become lately; how he'd shared his knowledge of jazz music, described his business deals, told her about his homes, and related anecdotes about famous people he knew—all without bragging!

He'd also talked about his charity work, particularly about the research foundation he'd created for hearing disorders, due to his sister's deafness. Best of all, he was willing to listen when she talked about Druradeen being more than just a place to live. She'd explained that the MacRoth tenants were all related by blood or marriage; that their homes and farms and shops had been passed down from generation to generation.

Rob began shaking his handsome head in dismay, and Duncan nearly sputtered with indignation. "You'll next be wanting to kiss his feet!" Duncan shouted. "Your kin will never forgive you if you let sentiment make you careless!"

"She won't do that," Rob interjected, but he continued to frown. He took Elgiva's hands. "Sister, don't you see what the man is doing? He's a master at charming people. He's simply changed his colors for the moment."

Elgiva shook her head. "I know that some of it is calculated. Believe me, he's a fair amazing actor, that one. But Rob, he's not a bad man. Maybe we've misjudged him."

"That's the end of it," Duncan snapped. "I'm taking you off the project. I'll substitute myself. And I promise you, by the end of the week the bastard will wish the last of his kin had died at the battle of

Talrigh, so that he himself would not be here to squirm."

Elgiva stepped close to the mayor and spoke right into his heavyset face. "You won't be threatening Mr. Kincaid!"

"You're infatuated with him! You're a traitor to your own clan!"

Rob angled between them and lifted a commanding hand. "Ellie, do you forget that you're speaking to the village mayor?" He glared at Duncan. "And you, you're addressing the next heir of MacRoth. Don't make ugly and foolish accusations."

Elgiva laid a hand on Rob's arm, half in apology, half to calm him down. Duncan snorted in disgust but said nothing, which was the closest he would ever come to admitting his own fault. Rob looked down at her with grave concern. "Don't become dazzled by Kincaid, Ellie. He's naught but a reiver."

She stepped back, furious. "I'll prove his change of heart to you. I'll get him to accept and acknowledge his Scot heritage. I'll have him wearing the tartan of Kincaid in two days' time. I'll have a statement signed by him, saying that he'll give up his option to buy the district. Then can we let him go?"

"I'll give you *one* day to accomplish this miracle," Duncan told her. "When you radio Rob tomorrow at midnight, I'll expect results, or your chance is ended. Kincaid stays penned up."

Elgiva nodded to Duncan, then kissed her brother's cheek. "He won't disappoint us, Robbie," she whispered, and she believed the words with her whole heart.

Douglas had just finished exercising when she returned from her meeting. Shom bounded up from the hearth rug and ran over to greet her, golden tail fanning the air. The sight of Douglas, half-dressed, smiling, and also happy to see her, made small agonies twist her insides. If she succeeded with his change of heart, he'd go free very soon. He'd be happy—so happy that she doubted he'd prosecute her for the kidnapping.

He'd go back to his glittering world, and she'd only see him in photographs or being interviewed on television. One day she'd see him with his blond, blue-eyed, sapphire-bedecked, intelligent, business-brilliant wife.

If she didn't succeed, he'd remain a prisoner, almost certainly growing bitter as the deadline for his real estate option passed. He'd hate her again and want revenge. Either way, she'd lose him. But the first option would be better for the MacRoth clan, she hoped.

"What's wrong?" he asked, as she wearily hung her cape on the hearth peg. "You look upset."

"Och. The weather is worse than an Englishman's temper today. I walked too far in it, that's all."

"Why don't you just fix sandwiches for supper?" He gave her an exaggerated leer. "And afterward come close to my parlor, fair Goldie, and I'll rub your tired feet."

Elgiva eyed him speculatively, considering which would be the best ways to persuade him. She also considered the erotic way in which he might massage her bare feet. "Aye, Kincaid, you've got a fair notion there. Sandwiches it is then. And how about a dram of whisky?"

"Aye, lassie, I'd love a snort."

After the light supper, she pulled her big chair near his bars. He pulled his chair close on the other side. Shom lay down between them. He didn't like to choose sides, she'd noticed. While sleet and fierce wind whipped the black night outside, Elgiva and Douglas toasted each other with glasses of whisky.

He downed his, set the glass aside, and slapped his thigh lustily. "Rest those bedraggled feet right here."

Elgiva gazed at him wistfully. In the light of a nearby lantern he looked so handsome. He wore the

silver-gray sweater, and the width of his shoulders
was emphasized against the shadowy background.
The lantern light gleamed on his black hair. His face
was a study in contrasts—strength and gentleness,
eagerness and contentment. The scar high on his
cheek was a sort of masculine beauty mark, she
decided. It drew her attention to his thickly lashed
eyes.

"You're staring at me, Goldie," he protested softly.
"Your feet, remember?"

"Oh. Would you do me a small favor tonight,
Douglas?"

He gestured around his cell. "My kingdom is yours."

"Would you listen if I read aloud? It's a grand
night for stories, and I'd like to read some of the old
Scottish legends." She held up both hands in a ca-
joling attitude. "You've naught to fear of a lecture
from me. But they're marvelous old stories."

His dark, intense eyes studied her without blinking. She held her breath. Finally he smiled a little
and nodded. "Give me your feet, and I'll give you my
ears."

When her bare feet lay in his lap and a book of
ancient ballads lay in her lap, she had trouble con-
centrating on the ballads and not her toes. He
wrapped his hands around them and stroked the
tops with sly, provocative movements. It was amazing that toes could radiate such erotic sensations.

Elgiva sank lower into her chair, her muscles loose
and her nerves tickling with pleasure. She opened
the old book with the languorous distraction of a
sleepwalker and stared blankly at a page.

"Read to me," he urged in a low, coaxing tone, as
if the request concerned a much more personal
entertainment.

Elgiva cleared her throat and forced herself to
begin. In a soft, melodic voice she recited "The Strik-
ing of Tyrdoune," an epic poem. She read slowly, not
only because Douglas's caressing hands made her

feel groggy, but also because she had to translate the Gaelic into English.

She put as much drama into her tone as she could, knowing that his dramatic nature appreciated her efforts. She was right. As Elgiva whispered about the death of Sir Drury in battle and gravely intoned the wizardry of Halifax, she noticed that Douglas's hands slowed. He clasped her feet around the insteps and only his thumbs made small circles on the tender skin inside the arches.

She glanced up and found him listening with his head tilted to one side and his body posed forward slightly, so that her feet were nestled against his hard stomach. "Go on," he said immediately, after she wiggled her toes and lost her train of thought. "Reading," he elaborated, then glanced down at her feet with a knowing smile. "Keep it up."

Elgiva made a strangled sound of exasperation and returned to her stories. Her voice rose grandly for the wars and dipped seductively for the romances, became angry for the betrayals and light for the elfin mischief. She almost cried when she told how the Scottish clans were broken once and for all by the English at the battle of Culloden.

Elgiva was shivering by the time she reached the epic's victorious conclusion, with Scotland proud despite all its hardships. The fireplace had gone dark, with only a few embers left glowing from the logs. A small clock on the mantel struck an hour well past midnight.

Elgiva shut the book and anxiously raised her eyes to Douglas's face. His somber and thoughtful expression buoyed her hopes. "What are you thinking, Douglas? Is it not a grand history?"

He nodded, but arched one black brow. "What? No Kincaids? I expected you to sneak them in."

"I told you before, they were struck from history." She flipped through the book hurriedly. "But I'll find a mention of them in an old song—"

"Stop while you're ahead, Goldie." His voice was

clipped, but his hands apologized by stroking her ankles. Elgiva looked at him hopefully, but he shook his head. "There was never a clan of Kincaid. That's why there's nothing in your book about them. But thank you for the rest. It was wonderful."

She straightened and pulled her feet from Douglas's lap before his surprised hands could stop her. "Didn't my history lesson give you anything new to consider?"

He watched her closely, sensing her change in mood. In a careful, troubled voice he asked, "What would you think if I built a museum and cultural center in the village?"

Elgiva's hopes crashed. "That wasn't the intent of the lecture."

"Ah. It *was* propaganda then. Goldie, you don't have to sell me on preserving Scottish history. You won't believe me, but I'm not going to ruin things here. I'm just going to expose all their charms to the world."

" 'Exposing our charms' doesn't sound dignified." Elgiva knotted her fists in her lap. "Won't you consider some compromises, Douglas? Such as leaving everyone as they are?"

The astonishment on his rugged face slowly hardened to anger. "You want me to give up and go home and call it a compromise? I tell you what. I'll buy the estate but I'll guarantee the tenants five years to find new homes, and I'll give each one a generous resettlement allowance. *And*, you can stay permanently. Rent free."

Elgiva leapt up. "You've been fooling me this past week! I thought you were becoming reasonable!"

"To agree to what you want, doll, I'd have to become senile!"

"You haven't softened a bit!"

"I *could* soften, if you'd open this damned cell door. I could forget the part you played in this stupid attempt at coercion."

"I've asked no mercy from you. I want nothing

from you but what your cruel Kincaid pride won't give."

He got to his feet also, looking frustrated. "I've always appreciated people who risk everything for their personal code of honor. I like to think that I'm that way, myself. But unless you let me go soon, you won't get out of this mess unhurt."

The cold threat in his voice sent chills down her spine. "Spoken like a mad dog, Kincaid," Elgiva retorted. "You deserve to wear the colors of your kin."

She ran to a chest in one corner and shoved the heavy, curved lid open. From inside Elgiva withdrew a magnificent tartan drape. The plaid was dark blue, gray, and white—the colors she'd given him to wear in his sweaters.

Elgiva strode to the cell and shoved the drape at him. He caught it and stared at her in fierce bewilderment. "That's what you should be proud of, Douglas! That's the tartan of the Kincaids. I made it for you myself—a great honor, considering how I feel about your clan! They wore that plaid through all the centuries that they protected their homeland. It could be said of us Scots that no matter how much we fought among ourselves, we always banded together to protect each other from outsiders."

Struggling not to cry with rage, she yelled, "Wear that plaid when you destroy what generations of Kincaids wouldn't dare to hurt!" She pivoted and went to the hearth. Shom followed, his tail drooping. She snatched her cape from the hearth peg.

"When you can't admit defeat, you run away," Douglas protested. "You'd rather walk the moors than stay here and fight."

She whirled around at the door to the front room. "I'm running from my sadness," she told him, her voice strained. "Because I wanted to think the best about you."

He looked at the window near the fireplace. The wind whipped a mixture of sleet and rain against the panes. "If you're determined to freeze to death, don't take Sam with you."

Elgiva tried to ignore the sting of those callous words. She would no longer expect cooperation, sympathy, or honor from Douglas Kincaid. She whipped the cape around herself. "Shom, stay." The big dog whimpered but sat down.

Kincaid slung the tartan onto his bed. "*Elgiva*, stay! Come back here and fight, you coward."

She stared at him in shock. "How do you know my first name?"

"Sam stole your mittens for me! He also brought me your diary. You must have suspected that I'd read it, but you didn't say anything. You're glad that I found out how you feel about me! Admit it. You want to be with me, and to hell with what happens to the rest of the MacRoths!"

"I'd rather die! You can dance on my grave!"

She left the cottage and strode into the brutal night. Bitter, she wondered if only foolish hearts and people unhappily in love were willing to brave the darkness outside rather than examine the darkness within.

Six

Elgiva would not leave him there to starve. He'd bet his life on her honor. In effect, he *had* bet his life on it.

By dawn Douglas's anger gave way to disbelief and then to alarm. Either she was punishing him and would return when he had shivered and gone hungry for a few hours more, or something had happened to her. He found himself worrying more about her well-being than about his own predicament.

Sam had waited patiently as long as he could; now he was desperate to go outside for reasons that had nothing to do with either Douglas or Elgiva's problems. He sat by the cell, looking up at Douglas urgently and wagging his tail.

Douglas shook his head. "You're on your own, boy. You've got my permission to decorate the front room to your heart's desire." Douglas waved a hand in that direction. "Go."

Sam ran to the other room, but years of strict training were too much for him to ignore. Douglas heard him scratching at the outer door. Surprisingly, the door creaked open. Douglas clasped the cell bars and listened, thinking that Elgiva had returned. But the sound of Sam's galloping paws disappeared into the sleet-streaked morning, and Douglas heard the unlocked door squeak as it swung back and forth on its hinges.

Where was Elgiva? He stared at the ugly weather outside the cottage window. She was probably drinking tea at a little highland inn somewhere, drinking tea and laughing about his misery. He cursed his concern for her and pulled the tartan closer around his shoulders. The cottage was freezing cold. He wouldn't forgive her for this little torture scheme.

Douglas lifted the end of the tartan drape and gazed at it in bitter consternation. Of course she was lying about there being a Kincaid clan. He studied the material closer, noting the skillfully woven cloth and perfect handwork around the edges. Doubt nagged at him. She'd gone to a lot of trouble to make him believe a lie.

What if nouveau riche Douglas Kincaid, a poor kid from the streets of Chicago, actually had a heritage that rivaled the proudest and the oldest in the Anglo-Saxon world?

He shook the sentimental thought away and began roaming around his cell again. An hour later Sam returned at a gallop and crashed to an undignified stop against the bars. He threw his head back and barked like an addled puppy.

"Quiet," Douglas ordered. Soft yips replaced the barking. Sam rose and planted his front paws on the cross bars. His whole body wiggled with impatience, and he looked at Douglas with pleading eyes.

Douglas stared at him worriedly. "Did you find her? Is something wrong with Elgiva?"

Sam howled. Douglas didn't know if the retriever's strange behavior had anything to do with Elgiva's disappearance, but it seemed likely. He looked around desperately, then snapped a hand toward the fireplace poker. "Fetch!"

On the stone wall of his cell was a rectangle of mortar and new rock where the window had been filled. Perhaps he could chip through it. Sam scrambled over to the poker, bumping a footstool on the hearth. The stool crashed to its side. A small drawer popped open under the upholstered top.

Out fell a large ring bearing a key.

After a stunned second, Douglas pointed at it instead. "Fetch! Get the key ring, Sam! The key ring!"

Sam brought the footstool, dragging it by one leg.

Douglas took a calming breath and pointed toward the hearth again. "Fetch!"

Sam brought a piece of firewood.

After five more tries, Sam brought the ring. Douglas took it, reached around the bars of the cell door, and slid the key into the lock. With a soft, well-oiled click, it turned. Douglas rammed the door with his shoulder. It snapped open.

For the first time in almost two hundred and seventy years, a Kincaid was free on the moors of Talrigh. In the best tradition of his ancestors, he immediately went to hunt down a MacRoth.

Half-conscious from fatigue and exposure, Elgiva barely knew when Sam returned. He had come once before, she remembered dimly, as she lifted her head from the soggy ground. Her head bumped a tree limb and she winced in discomfort. The drenched hood of her cape clung to the sides of her face like blinders. Her forehead met Sam's cold, inquisitive nose and warm tongue.

"Shom," she croaked, wondering how he'd gotten out of the cottage, but too weary to care. She rested her head on the icy, matted grass again.

Suddenly Sam's snuffling nose was replaced by a hand that jerked her hood back and checked the pulse point on the side of her throat. Elgiva frowned in groggy confusion.

The hand left. Someone began tugging on the tree limbs that pinned her down. Didn't the someone know that it was a good-sized tree that no person of ordinary strength could budge? Hadn't she tried for hours to crawl out from under it?

This someone was obviously not ordinary, because the tree began to move. Elgiva stirred weakly and tried to shift her numb, water-logged body. Soaked with rain, the wool cape was a mantel of lead that clung to her possessively.

The hand returned. It brought a second hand with it. Together they pulled her from under the limbs and turned her to lay on her back. She covered her eyes against the sleet. A long, thick arm went under her shoulders and pulled her upward, then cradled her head against a broad chest. The hand pushed her matted hair back and stroked her face with gentle fingers.

Elgiva squinted up to see if she could recognize the good Scot who'd come to her rescue. Instead she found the rain-slicked frown of Douglas Kincaid.

From her garbled description Douglas finally determined that as she had walked through the small ravine last night, the tree had fallen from a soggy bank above her. When he explained the method of his escape, she watched him with grim, exhausted eyes.

Carrying her, he headed back to the cottage. Douglas kept glancing down at her, fear a tight knot inside his chest. Her fair complexion was ashen, her lips blue. Her hands shook violently and her teeth chattered even though he'd wrapped her in the tartan drape he'd been wearing.

They were nearly two miles from the cottage. Douglas had to stop and rest for a minute during the long trek back. Sitting down on an outcrop of rock, he tucked the tartan closer around her. His breath shuddered from more than exertion—what if she were seriously hurt? Though the sleet had made a wet, icy prison of his sweater and trousers, he shivered because of what she'd suffered during the past six hours. He lifted her and walked on, Sam trotting beside him.

"I w—weigh almost t—twelve s—stone," she whispered. "Y—you c—can't carry me the whole w—way."

"Since I don't know how much twelve stone is or are, you're in luck."

"N—not l—luck." Her voice was woozy and weak. "F—failed. All is l—lost."

"Well, that's gratitude for you. Do I look as if I'm escaping? You don't see me running off and leaving you to freeze, do you?"

"N—no g—good to you f—frozen. N—no revenge in t—that."

"Right. I want you alive and worried senseless about what I'm going to do to you. Now pipe down."

He held her a little closer to his chest and angled his head over hers to protect her face from the sleet. This was an unusual and caring form of revenge, and they both knew it.

Shock and defeat crouched in the back of her mind like wolves waiting to attack, but Elgiva was too dazed to acknowledge them. Every bone in her body seemed to be rattling against the others, and only one thought penetrated the fog in her mind: She had to get warm.

Once inside the cottage Douglas lowered her to the hearth and quickly built a fire. While he ran to turn up the gas heaters, she tried to stretch her hands toward the flames, but her strength gave out and she tumbled sideways. Sam, dripping wet and cold himself, flopped across her and licked her face.

Immediately Douglas returned, pushing Sam away and lifting her into a sitting position again. He stripped her cape off and looked at the soggy sweater and skirt underneath. Elgiva heard him mutter something dark and anxious sounding. *He's afraid,* she noted in amazement. She'd never imagined him being worried for her sake.

She smiled at him groggily as he undressed her. One minute she was sitting on the hearth encased in freezing, wet wool; the next she was sitting on the hearth stark naked, and Douglas was scrubbing her with a towel. He carried her to bed and shoved her under the covers, for which she was ecstatically grateful. She made soft, mewling sounds of appreciation and burrowed into a cocoon of feather mattress and muslin sheets.

Not long afterward her cocoon was invaded by a second caterpillar.

Elgiva hesitated, then gave up and huddled against Douglas's body. He wrapped his arms around her. She didn't mind that he was naked too. He was fantastically warm and furry, and that was all that mattered when her teeth were clattering like castanets.

He threw a leg over her and drew her against his torso and thighs. The heat began to return to her skin as he rubbed her back and buttocks vigorously. Grasping her hands from where she'd tucked them against his chest, he blew on the icy fingers, then impatiently shoved all four fingers of one hand into his mouth and sucked them for a minute. He repeated the technique on the fingers of the other hand, and Elgiva decided with fuzzy objectivity that her fingers now felt wonderful.

"Get into your tent," he ordered gruffly, and from somewhere he produced her nightgown. Elgiva refused to lift her arms from the sheltering heat of his body, so finally he slid the gown over her head and pulled it down, leaving her arms inside.

Abruptly he dove under the covers. Elgiva had her legs drawn up. He curved himself around them and nestled her chilled feet into the hollow of his stomach. Her shivering toes curved downward, and he jerked them up again. She heard a muffled protest, something about his Popsicle.

As he scrubbed sensation back into her feet she bit her lip to keep from crying out in pain. Finally he covered them with a pair of her bulky wool socks, and she relaxed as if unwound.

He stretched out beside her again. She felt his

fingers stroking her face, then his breath as he blew on her skin. When he warmed the tip of her nose between his lips, she opened her eyes and stared at him in sleepy, nearly cross-eyed fascination. True to Douglas Kincaid's nature, his first aid techniques were commanding and bawdy, but irresistible.

He rubbed a towel over her head, then bundled it around her damp hair. She felt his tongue covering each of her earlobes with delicious heat. Elgiva sighed when he put his arms around her again and angled one leg between her knees. His mouth touched hers; he kissed her very gently, then pulled her head into the crook of his neck.

"I'm in charge now, and you're in deep trouble," he whispered.

"I know," she mumbled, and fell peacefully asleep.

The extent of her trouble dawned on her hours later, when she woke up. A dull sense of dread crept into her thoughts as strength returned. Douglas had escaped. He could do what he wanted with her inheritance and with her. Elgiva opened her eyes and peeked groggily over the covers. She was alone in bed.

She'd slept all day. A dark night had settled outside the window beside the hearth, and shadows danced on the walls from the fire. Sam was curled up on the hearth rug. She heard sounds in the kitchen and smelled the fantastic aroma of hot food.

Douglas came into the room carrying a large bowl and a spoon. He was wearing his red long johns. She felt a twinge of guilt, recalling that she'd chosen them to ridicule and humble him. However, there was nothing ridiculous or humble about the way Douglas Kincaid filled the clinging garment.

Quivers ran through her as she thought of his nakedness earlier and the lusty methods he had used to warm her. He saw her staring at him and sat down close to her on the bed, his eyes troubled as they searched her face.

He held the bowl on one knee and cupped a caressing hand against her cheek. "How do you feel? Have you thawed out?"

"Aye. I'm fine." Questions were trapped in her throat. She struggled to ask them but couldn't.

He shook his head at her efforts. "Have some supper. A Kincaid special. Canned soup fresh from the can. Heated to perfection over a hot burner."

Elgiva sat up in bed and arranged the pillows behind herself. With her hair streaming in a shaggy mop over her shoulders, she felt like a hag. Why was Douglas looking at her as if she were the prettiest woman he'd ever seen? She leaned back and accepted the spoonfuls of delicious beef and vegetables that he lifted to her mouth. He dabbed one finger under her lip, caught a drop of broth, then brought the finger to his tongue. "Hmmm. Soup du Elgiva."

She grasped his forearm and gazed into his eyes with agonized uncertainty. "What now, Douglas?"

"How about a cup of tea? And we have some oatmeal cookies left from yesterday."

She shook his arm in rebuke and repeated grimly, "What now?"

He set the soup bowl aside and clasped her face between his hands. "Somehow we'll work things out. We'll find a way. But not tonight. We're both too emotional right now. I don't want to argue about the future tonight, doll. Just trust me—there *will* be a future, and it will be happy."

Her breath fluttered in her throat. Stunned, she studied his eyes and saw the unmistakable concern and sincerity there. She wanted so much to trust him. She wanted so much to believe that there might be a future with him. If he cared about her at all, he'd do the right thing for her home and her kin.

If he cared about her even a wee bit as much as she cared about him, she'd never regret her decision.

Elgiva threw herself against his chest and kissed

him, distraught and awkward with her arms still trapped in her gown. Douglas responded as if she'd done the most seductive thing in the world. He whispered her name and pulled her across his lap in a fierce embrace.

Elgiva felt senseless with tender lust; she wanted to touch him everywhere and make him happy; she wanted to smile and cry and hug him until her arms ached; she wanted to feel his hands on her skin and watch his eyes as he lost control. She put all her energy into nuzzling and kissing him.

"El. El. My God," he said in soft amazement, sounding pleased. Then he probbed her mouth with his tongue, showing how a kiss could imitate the greatest intimacies, how it could make her womb loosen with delicious heat and her legs feel weak.

Rivers of desire ran through her body every time he moved his mouth in a new way or caressed her through the nightgown. His hands slid down to her hips, then over her thighs. He touched her to give pleasure, and he knew where his touch could provoke it most.

Before she'd met him, Elgiva had pictured the great Douglas Kincaid as a selfish lover, the kind of man who would demand his own satisfaction first, as he did in the business world. Now she knew that he wasn't that way at all, and like so many puzzles about him, it both elated and frightened her. How could she ever control him if he kept surprising her?

Elgiva brushed her lips across his face, exploring his cheeks and jaw with slow kisses. He dipped his head and caught the skin beneath her ear in his teeth without hurting her. Slowly his teeth and lips journeyed lower, finally reaching the pulse point at the base of her neck.

When he'd dressed her earlier, he hadn't buttoned her gown. Now he burrowed his face between the open neckline and sucked the base of her throat lightly, making her pulse throb. The action released waves of languor in her mind. Her eyes half-shut, she vaguely knew that she was rubbing her cheek against his head with the ecstasy of a purring cat.

Elgiva struggled to put her arms through the nightgown's sleeves; his hands rose to her chest and slid under the neckline, making it gape across her breasts. He raised his head and seared her with a look that was both greedy and restrained.

Elgiva gasped softly at the power in it. Had she ever had control of this man, even when he was behind bars? At the moment control seemed very unimportant.

"Oh, help me take this gown off," she begged, almost crying. "And you get undressed too. You said once that there were better ways to keep warm. Prove it to me, Douglas. Prove it."

Delight blazed in his eyes. With a gruff sound of approval he lifted the gown over her head. Elgiva put her hands, trembling, on the tiny red buttons down the center of his long johns.

He tossed the gown on the floor, then grasped her arms and studied her with obvious approval, his lips parted in a slight smile. Lifting one hand, he trailed the backs of his fingers over her breasts and belly, then stroked her thighs. He twirled a finger into the soft mat of chestnut hair between them.

"This isn't enough fur to keep you from catching cold, big girl." His teasing voice held a low rumble of passion that curled around her senses.

"Let me see if *your* fur keeps you warm enough," she whispered. Elgiva unfastened his buttons, noting breathlessly that his chest moved faster each time she pushed a bit more material aside. The buttons continued to the bottom of his belly.

So did Elgiva.

The darkly haired skin and thick muscles of his abdomen quivered when she brushed her fingertips across them. She slowly, carefully parted the soft red cloth and studied him. She put her fingers out and traced the streak of silver hair from where it started at the center of his chest to where it ended, making a silver background for an even more fascinating attraction.

Elgiva hesitated, desperate to hold him but afraid that she'd do something dramatically embarrassing. Jonathan had never wanted to be caressed like this.

Douglas raised a hand to her face. "Look at me, Elgiva." She lifted her gaze and saw a question in his eyes. He traced her lips with the edge of his forefinger and said quaintly, "It's a work of art, I know, but some men want their lovers to do more than just admire it. I happen to be that kind of man. Anything done gently will be appropriate."

She relaxed and smiled at him. He seemed to understand. "Like this?"

As her fingers caressed inside his clothes he shuddered and kissed her deeply, thrusting his tongue against hers and growling gently when she returned the action. "Hmmm huh," was the only response he could manage, but it made her bold.

Elgiva slid both hands over him, reveling in the amazing variety of textures. She pushed the long johns off his shoulders and molded her fingers to the sheathed mounds of muscle and sinew there. She could barely concentrate because his hands were performing a similar magic on her body, finding every secret route to their ultimate destination.

He paused, his hands cupped possessively over the junction of her hips and thighs. Her eyes were shut, but she sensed his gaze on her face. She met his troubled scrutiny. "You're not afraid of me, are you?" he murmured. "You don't have to do this just because I escaped."

Her breath made a ragged sound as she inhaled. "I am afraid of you. But I think you're a wee bit afraid of me too. Maybe we can stop scaring each other if we do this . . . this . . . I don't know what you call this, but I can only call it making love."

His soft chuckle contrasted with a somber nod of his head. "Nothing and no one can stop me from doing something that seems so right. And yes, I want to call it 'making love' too."

Elgiva laughed shakily. "Then let's give it a try."

Moving in unspoken harmony, she lay back as he finished removing the long johns. Elgiva gazed avidly at the strong, broad expanse of his back and the sleek grace of his buttocks. His thighs were sculpted; thick but lean and corded where they joined his body. His sex was truly a work of art; it made her hands quiver at the memory of soft, hot skin and the hardness it covered.

He stretched out close beside her and cupped the back of her head. When he smiled, she pulled him to her demanding mouth and made their earlier kisses seem innocent by comparison. Elgiva arched under the slow stroking of his hand, her body opening as if fully ripe for the first time in her life.

She quivered and cried out in pleasure. So this was the way a man should touch a woman, she thought with a flicker of sadness. She had missed even more than she'd realized all these years.

"What's wrong, sweet doll?" Douglas asked hoarsely, his lips moving against hers. "Why are there tears in your eyes?"

She wondered why she'd ever considered him insensitive. "I've waited a long time, that's all," she said vaguely. When he frowned in bewilderment, Elgiva forced a small, jaunty smile. "Almost two weeks."

He shook his head, and she knew that he saw more to her pensiveness than that. "I've waited too. What's really wrong?"

"Nothing. I just . . . don't want to wait any longer. Please, Douglas. Now."

"Sssh. All right. Whatever you want, El." He drew her closer and carefully moved atop her. "Whatever you need."

She smiled tearfully. "Dear man, talking that way will get you in trouble that no negotiation can settle."

"I love trouble. I love being here with you."

They kissed urgently, while their bodies settled into a position as ancient as the first dreams shared by a man and a woman. Elgiva's senses flooded with millions of stars; desire calmed her, released her, made nothing seem more important than the second when she lifted herself and met him, taking him in with a silken welcome that made him groan and smile at the same time. He arched against her and completed the moment.

They trembled with shared energy and emotion. He moved his larger, heavier form against her with a finesse that pressed her deeply into the bed without crushing her; she gave him her softest, most vulnerable self but made him understand that he shouldn't hold anything back.

The kaleidoscope of emotions shifted with the merest signal; new patterns flowered from the changing expressions deep in his eyes and each new attitude of his mouth. She guided him with her sighs and the grip of her legs; with her hands as she dragged them down his back or skimmed the flexing muscles of his hips.

She put her fingertips alongside his face and asked him for time with just that slight hold. He understood immediately and slowed his rhythm, watching her through heavy-lidded eyes filled with need and affection. Her desire became frantic exhilaration, and all she could do was chant his name, then smile, then laugh brokenly.

He covered her face with kisses and surged faster against her. She became somber, stunned by the pleasure rising inside her again. Intense emotions suffused his expression. His mouth was tight with passion but also contentment. Then he winked at her, and it was as if he had said, We're the only two people who know how wonderful this is.

I love you so much, Elgiva thought with an aching swell of emotion. It overwhelmed reason and fear, but she didn't care. She burrowed her head into the crook of his neck and held his shoulders tightly while he whispered praises against his ear.

Elgiva moaned as he unleashed his restraint, finally letting himself go beyond control into a fervor that ended with a soft shout followed by her murmured name. Nothing had ever sounded so sweet to her.

They held each other tightly during the satiated stillness that followed, their faces nuzzled together, their mouths seeking quick kisses between hurried breaths. Elgiva adored the hot pulse of his body inside hers, and she was awed by the perfect feeling of trust and unity.

She made a sound of protest when he lifted his torso on braced elbows. But he merely positioned himself where he could study her face. "You are the most incredible woman," he said gruffly.

Her eyes burned with tears of joy. "Did you know that once you've kissed a fairy you can never go back to the real world?"

He smiled tenderly. "Some day we're going to have to discuss the term 'fairy' and what it meant where I grew up." When she gave him a puzzled look, he shook his head. "I'll take my chances in *Elf-hame.* Hmmm." His voice dropped to a throaty invitation. "Or maybe I'll convince the fairy to come to the real world with me."

"I don't think that's how it works." Elgiva slid her toes up and down the backs of his legs, then decided to ensure his staying. She wrapped her legs around him and locked her ankles together. Somehow she'd win him. Somehow she'd keep him.

"A prisoner again," he muttered gravely, arching one brow.

"Aye. Make the best of it."

He lowered himself and began kissing her. They sighed at the same time and shared a look of quiet ecstasy. "I will make the best of it," he promised, and once again, he did.

•　•　•

Douglas woke up sometime after midnight, jarred by Elgiva's absence from bed. He sat up quickly and rubbed a hand over his eyes, then exhaled with relief when he saw her kneeling on the hearth. She was dressed in her frumpy gown and robe, and she was placing new logs on the fire. Sam lay beside her, yawning.

The emotions that swirled inside his chest finally merged into coherent thought. *Trapped inside all that practical cloth is the most giving, the most sensual woman in the world.* Now he understood why he loved to watch her, even when she was doing something as mundane as building a fire or reading one of her musty-looking books. She was suffused with quiet passion, an unapologetic enjoyment of food and making love and the simple pleasures of life. He loved her contentment.

Excited plans began to form as he studied her. It would be fantastic to please her with gifts beyond her wildest dreams. He'd buy the MacRoth estate and give her all the money she needed to renovate the shabby manor hall. She'd love that. She'd love *him*.

"I know a better way to keep warm," Douglas called softly.

She twisted from the fireplace in a quick, almost guilty way. Douglas smiled at her in bewilderment. "Elgiva?"

She stood and hurried over to him, dispelling his concern with a glowing smile. She took his outstretched hands and sat down close to his torso, curling her legs under her. But her hands were cold and damp. He studied her intently. "Are you feeling all right?"

She started to speak, hesitated, then looked away, as if listening. She shook her head and sighed. When her eyes met his again, they were troubled, and her smile was gone. "We need to talk, dear man."

Douglas brought her hands to his mouth and kissed them. "I think it can wait. I promise you, everything will be all right." He cupped her hands to his mouth and shut his eyes. She stroked his jaw, and he nodded happily.

"Please, we have to talk," she said again. "Would you mind getting dressed?" She pointed to the trousers and sweater she'd draped across the foot of the bed. "I'd like you to come and sit beside the fire."

More bewildered than ever, Douglas tried to coax her into relaxing. "El," he murmured, putting a little rebuke into it. He lifted the covers invitingly and watched her gaze dart to his naked body. "Get undressed and come back to bed, El," he urged. "And we'll talk all night."

She chuckled, but the sound was worried. "It's not talking we'd be doing."

"El, do we have to discuss the estate's future right now?"

"No, not that. Something else. Would you please get dressed?"

He saw the tension in the set of her shoulders and the solemn attitude of her mouth. Elgiva MacRoth was one no-nonsense lady. Douglas intended to teach her the pleasures of being impractical. But he was patient.

Douglas sat up and held out his arms. "How about a hug to warm me up before I get out of bed?"

She looked distressed but snuggled into his arms, resting her head on his shoulder. He stroked her hair. "Name something you'd really like to have, El. Something that's not the least bit practical. Something you've never thought that you could have. Something you want simply because it would make you happy."

"Children," she said in a tormented voice.

Shaken, he wished he'd been more specific and saved her from such sorrow. *Yeah, Kincaid,* he said to himself. *Explain that you meant the important stuff. Jewelry. Cars. Money.* Douglas kissed the top of her head. "Are you certain that you can't have children?"

"No, but it seems likely. Jonathan was as healthy as a horse. And all of his brothers had children."

"Did you and Jonathan ever see a doctor about the problem?"

"No. Jonathan wouldn't go. It shamed him, he said. If we weren't meant to have any bairns, then that was that. What point was there in learning whose fault it was?"

Douglas gritted his teeth at such backwardness. "Didn't he wonder if the problem could be corrected with medical help?"

"No. He was a proud man. He was a shy man. And as I said, the problem was likely mine. I didn't want to know the truth either. We were married for life, children or not. Why be humiliated when it would change naught?" Her hands clasped his and clenched them tightly. "I think you're safe, Douglas. You don't have to worry about becoming a father from tonight's frolic, if that's why you're asking."

Douglas drew back. She looked at him carefully. He glared at her. "Dammit, do you really believe that's why I'm asking?"

Her face went pale. "I don't know! I'm sorry. I'm a wee bit distracted right now. *Please* get dressed. Then we can talk some more."

He shook her lightly. "What's wrong with you? Why are you upset?"

"Because you won't do me the simple favor of covering your handsome behind and coming to sit by the fire! Is that too much to ask?"

She was trembling now. He stared hard into her golden eyes, and a terrible sense of foreboding swept over him. "Elgiva?" he said slowly, demanding explanations.

"Oh, Douglas, my dearest—" Her voice broke. Shaking her head, she raised both hands and stroked his face gently. "You've been so wonderful tonight. I wish it could go on forever."

"It can, El, it can."

Sam leapt up and ran to the outer room, growling.

Elgiva gasped and began tugging at Douglas's hands. "Get dressed! Oh, please, get dressed!"

Douglas stared at her in horrified understanding. "Someone's here," he accused numbly. "You set me up."

"No, I swear, I didn't mean it to be that way! I forgot to use the radio—you and I, we were busy, you remember, and then we fell asleep! And when I woke up, I remembered to call my people, but it was too late! They think something's gone wrong!"

Sam was barking ferociously now. Bitter with betrayal, Douglas pushed Elgiva aside and grabbed his clothes. "I'm getting out of here and taking you with me, doll, and I'm going to make you wish you'd never played me for a fool."

"I wasn't trying to trap you again!"

"Save the lies for your fairy tales."

There was a crash as the door burst open in the other room. Elgiva started from the bed. Douglas snatched her to him, then pinned her around the waist with one arm. Sam backed into the room, snarling.

A half-dozen men burst in, carrying guns and walking sticks. They wore dark clothes and ski masks, but from the variety of old weapons and far-from-athletic bodies Douglas surmised that they weren't professionals at this kind of adventure.

"No, no, no!" Elgiva screamed as they surrounded the bed, guns pointing at Douglas's head. "Calm down!"

A tall, muscular man, apparently the leader and certainly the only one who looked both athletic and deadly, made a throaty sound of rage. "Let her go," he snarled at Douglas.

Douglas considered the fact that he was sitting in Elgiva's bed naked and that, quite possibly, the tall man was a close relative of Elgiva's. "I think she's all that stands between me and certain death," he observed. Douglas tightened his arm around Elgiva's middle. "I'm not going to hurt her. Back off."

"Please," Elgiva begged. "He's not going anywhere. Don't start a fight. Just make him go back to the cell."

"What has he done to you?" the leader asked in a thick Scottish burr. "If he's harmed you in any way, tell me."

"No, no, he hasn't done anything but escaped."

A man who looked like a fat, hooded wrestler brandished an old shotgun. "He escaped right to your bed, I see! And he looks to be at home there!"

"Is that true?" the tall man asked Elgiva, sounding distraught. "You didn't let the bastard out on purpose, did you?"

"No!"

"She did, she did!" the shorter man insisted. "I can see the guilty look on her face! She's betrayed us all!"

"Don't be a fool!" the other man retorted. "She's been forced into something, can't you see? And she knew we'd come when she didn't use the radio!"

"He escaped, but he stayed for my sake!" Elgiva cried. "I could have told him to run when I realized that you were on your way, but I didn't do it!"

Disappointment made a hard, unyielding fist in Douglas's chest. Loyalty and honesty were the two things he cherished most about his family, about *anyone* who became important to him. In a cutthroat world, he had to have that haven of trust, if only among a few people. Deep down he respected Elgiva's motivations, but her betrayal hurt.

"So you *did* trap me," Douglas said between gritted teeth.

He felt her shivering inside the circle of his arm. She turned her face toward him and a single tear slid down her cheek. "A wee bit," she admitted. "But only . . . later. What happened between us wasn't a cold-blooded calculation. I swear."

Douglas looked at the men grimly. "Hell, yes, she let me out," he told them. "She's seen how pointless your deal is, so she's changed sides. And we've spent

the past few hours playing hop-Scotch in bed together. So if you're going to lock me up again, you
better put Mata MacHari in the slammer with me."

Elgiva shrieked in distress. "He's twisting the truth!
He's just trying to cause trouble!"

The tall man thrust his rifle into the hands of a
companion. He advanced on the bed with both massive fists raised. "Pull on your pants, Kincaid, and
get out of bed. I'm about to beat you senseless."

Douglas grinned slowly. Elgiva twisted to look at
him with eyes full of desperation. "No! I won't have
you two kill each other! Please, Douglas, get back in
the cell! I'll get in there with you! Just stop this!
Stop it!"

"Stop it. My sentiments exactly," a new voice said
with calm authority. Everyone jumped. Douglas
looked toward the door to the outer room. There
stood T. S. Audubon, dressed like a commando in a
spy movie. Audubon's love for drama was in full
swing. He scowled grandly and waved an automatic
assault rifle that made all the combined weaponry in
the room look puny.

The window next to the hearth shattered as two of
Audubon's assistants poked their rifles inside. "If all
you gentlemen will drop your weapons and go over
to the cell, I'll be very happy," Audubon ordered.
"You really don't have any choice."

"Nice timing," Douglas commented.

"Thank you. Nice hostage you've got there."

"I might let her go if she'll tell her cronies to
cooperate. I'm sure she doesn't want any of their
plaid blood on her conscience."

"Especially since one of them is her brother,"
Audubon added.

Douglas felt Elgiva stiffen. "Go, please," she told
her accomplices, looking directly at their tall leader.
"We don't want anybody hurt because of my mistake."

The defeat in her voice made Douglas angrier. It
tore at his resolve not to feel any sympathy for her.
She'd deliberately kept him busy in bed, knowing

that the others would arrive to trap him again. He wasn't going to let himself forget that.

"I can't believe you betrayed us," Elgiva's brother accused bitterly. He removed his mask, exposing hair the same reddish-brown shade as hers and a face no less proud.

"I didn't do that," she murmured in a broken voice. "But maybe I made a mistake or two in judgment."

"Deceiving someone who wanted to treat you fairly is a *damned* bad mistake in judgment," Douglas told her.

"This is fair?" She looked down at his binding arm. "You didn't hesitate to think the worst of me and try to make my own people turn on me."

"Aye, 'tis an odd brand of fairness!" her brother shouted. "I'm thinking that my sister is innocent of all but trusting a man who knows how to charm people into heading for hell with him!"

"I'm sure that hell is a very profitable place," Douglas returned smoothly. "Why don't you go there and report back to me?"

Everyone tensed even more. Elgiva's brother lurched forward, but his companions grabbed his arms. The short, chubby man jerked his mask off also, revealing a florid face, red hair, and a calculated smile. "We don't want any trouble here, lads." Where he had been a troublemaker seconds earlier, he was now a diplomat. "Do as Mr. Audubon says. Let's put our guns down and move back."

"Nice change of heart, Mayor MacRoth," Audubon observed.

"Please, Rob," Elgiva begged, staring at her brother. "Do as they ask." His expression furious, he slowly complied, and the others followed. The room filled with Audubon's men, and they surrounded the kidnappers.

Audubon sighed with relief and pulled a dark knit cap off his head, then ran a hand through white hair that flowed to his shoulders. He stepped to the foot of Elgiva's bed.

Douglas was in too bad a mood to appreciate the way his friend smiled at the compromising scene there. "Well, Douglas, it looks as if you didn't need rescuing at all," Audubon noted dryly.

Douglas felt the rigid resistance in Elgiva's trapped body. "I needed all the help I could get," he answered.

And this was just the beginning.

Seven

Elgiva sat in her chair by the fireplace, staring stubbornly into space while self-rebuke and sorrow made a cold knot inside her stomach. Douglas and his henchmen had allowed her to pull on a pair of brown trousers and tuck her nightgown into them; because they wouldn't give her the privacy to change into other clothes, she looked ridiculous. She tossed her robe onto the floor and drew a black wool sweater over her bulging, clumsy gown.

Douglas, who was already dressed in his gray trousers and sweater, threw her walking shoes near the hearth. "Put them on," he said curtly.

Shom went to the shoes, took both into his mouth, and carried them the last bit of distance to her. Tears choked Elgiva's throat. She stroked Shom's head and wished humans could keep trust alive so faithfully.

Elgiva felt everyone in the room watching her as she stuffed her feet into the shoes. Rob, Duncan, Andrew, and the village physician, Dr. Graham, were locked in Douglas's cell along with the new men they'd brought with them. John Callum and Richard Maxwell were farmers—their families had lived on the MacRoth land for hundreds of years, passing their parcels down as if they owned them. John,

Richard, and the other farmers on the estate stood to lose as much of their heritage as the MacRoths did, if Douglas refused to change his plans.

Mr. Audubon and his men lounged around the cottage, looking glad to be out of the cold highland night. Douglas did not look glad about anything. He stood across the room with his legs braced and his arms crossed over his chest, eyeing Elgiva with unwavering dismay.

She raised her equally grim gaze to his. "I'll be going to the cell with my kin and my neighbors now. I'd like to be kept with them, if that's not too much to ask."

"I want information," Douglas retorted. "Who planned this kidnapping?"

"I did," Elgiva and Rob said in unison.

Elgiva pressed her hands to her throat. "Don't steal my thunder, Robbie! This was all my idea, and you know it!"

"No," Dr. Graham said sternly, his shaggy gray head shaking slowly. "The whole bunch of us planned it. And a dozen more besides. You reivers will have to prosecute the whole community or none at all!"

"Aye," Andrew said. He was a thin, wiry man who had never lost his military posture from a career in the British air force. Now he drew himself up proudly, as if he were about to be executed. "I flew everyone back and forth to America in my plane, and I flew the helicopter that stole you from your rooftop, Mr. Kincaid."

"And I fixed a cell in this place to hold you," Duncan announced.

"And I helped!" John Callum added.

"Myself also!" Richard Maxwell said.

"And it was me who researched everything about you," Rob told Douglas with smug victory. "You and your disgusting, self-indulgent life-style."

Elgiva buried her head in her hands. "You promised it wouldn't be this way, lads! We agreed that I'd be the one to take the blame! I don't have children to leave behind! Or a mate! Do you not see how you've hurt your families, you proud fools?"

"Ellie, I haven't got children or a mate, either," Rob reminded her. She heard the apology in his voice and knew that he was sorry for accusing her of betrayal earlier.

"But you would have had them eventually," she told him, lifting her head to offer him a gaze of tormented affection. "You had more of a future to lose than I did. All I had was my shop—"

"Enough!" Douglas said loudly. Elgiva looked at him and found his expression darker than ever. Was there also a hint of surprise and distress in it? Perhaps remorse? She was too wounded to trust her hopes right now.

He slashed the air with one hand. "I want the truth. What did you people expect to get from me? Why didn't you try to bargain?"

"With the man who never bargains unless it serves him best? The man who tried to copyright his own name so that no other could use it in business? The man who once evicted all the old people from a nursing home so that he could build a parking lot for his office building?"

Douglas shook his head. "You don't know the truth."

Elgiva went on raggedly, her hands digging into the arms of her chair. "We had naught to bargain with, Douglas! Just our traditions! Just our legends! Just our love for our homes! What would that mean to a man such as yourself, who judges everything by its price in money?"

"Aye, 'tis a sad state, even for a Kincaid," Rob taunted.

The others began nodding and talking all at once. "Aye, a Kincaid! Even for a Kincaid! You'd think he'd have a drop of his ancestors' loyalty to hearth and kin! We didn't want to have a Kincaid for our laird, but a *loyal* Kincaid would have been—"

"What is this?" Douglas yelled. "Are all of you

going to push this bogus 'clan of Kincaid' story to save your hides? If so, forget it!"

Elgiva stood, her shoulders squared, and faced her fellow kidnappers resolutely. "He doesn't believe," she told them. "It's useless to discuss what he won't listen to. And if he did, what's to say he'd change his mind about buying the MacRoth holdings? No, let's talk to him in the only way he'll consider. Let's bargain using something that he really wants."

"This ought to be interesting," Audubon interjected.

Elgiva faced Douglas's stern scrutiny. "My brother and I are the MacRoth heirs, but I'm the eldest, and I'm the one who kept you prisoner. Can't you have me arrested and let the others go?"

Loud protests rose from the group in the cell, led by Rob's shouts of disapproval. Douglas clasped his hands behind his back and waited with a taut look of patience on his face until everyone quieted. "I won't have you arrested the way your martyred self would love," he mocked lightly. "Instead I'll take you with me."

"You won't do it!" Rob yelled.

Elgiva's relief mingled with dread. "To where?" she asked numbly.

"To wherever I feel like," he retorted.

"For what purpose?"

"For whatever I feel like."

Rob shook the cell bars. "I say no! No!"

Her pulse racing, Elgiva studied Douglas's eyes. She nodded toward her brother and the others. "And they'll go free? And you promise not to take any other action against them? Or against anyone else but me?"

He nodded. "I swear it."

"So be it, then. I'll do whatever you say."

"Elgiva," Rob protested in helpless fury.

She gripped the back of the chair for support but kept unyielding eyes on the man who now held her future in his vengeful grasp. "He's not a bad man, Rob," she said, never taking her eyes from Douglas.

"He only covets what he can't possess easily. Now that he's got me, he'll let me go soon. You'll see."

"I'll let you go when it suits me," Douglas said with a thin, cool smile. "And it won't be until after I've bought the MacRoth estate."

She forced a shrug. "Just keep to your word about not sending anyone else to jail."

"Oh, I will." Authoritative and brusque, he turned toward Audubon. "You witnessed all this. Elgiva MacRoth and I have an agreement."

The enigmatic Audubon merely sighed. "It's the strangest thing I've seen in years, but yes, consider me an official witness to the deal."

"Let's get out of here, then."

Elgiva's nerves jumped. "I want my people turned loose first!"

"You're in no position to give orders," Douglas informed her.

"When we get to Druradeen, we'll send someone back to open the cell door," Audubon said. He turned to gaze drolly at Duncan. "I'll speak to the mayor's mother about it. I'm sure she'll know who to send. I'm curious, mayor. What part did your mother play in the kidnapping? Was she the decoy in New York?"

"Aye. She distracted Kincaid's security people so that Elgiva could sneak into his New Year's Eve party," Duncan said smugly. "She pretended to faint in the lobby of his skyscraper. Aye, not even the employees of the coldhearted Kincaid could resist a wee old lady with a dizzy spell."

Elgiva met Douglas's eyes again and found them dully amused. The humor died quickly and was replaced by determination. "Congratulations for your deception," he told her. "Now you're going to pay for it."

"Stop threatening, Douglas, and get on with it. If we're going, let's go."

"Ellie," Rob called. She hurried to the cell, her vision suddenly blinded by tears. He took her hands, and they shared a long, intense gaze. They put their heads together, and she spoke to him in Gaelic. "He's a good man, Robbie. I'll be safe with him."

"How can you say that, sister?"

She gazed up at Rob with absolute conviction. "Because I love him, and I know his heart."

Rob's eyes widened with amazement. "Does he love you?"

She shook her head, thinking of petite blondes with all sorts of worldly business and social skills; blondes with blue eyes suited to sapphires; blondes who could bear children. Then she drew Rob's hands through the bars and kissed the back of each.

She looked at him calmly. "But he won't harm me. The only way Douglas could harm me would be if he said that he loved me, too, and it was a lie. I'm sure he'll let me go soon. Perhaps I can soften him toward our inheritance. Who knows? But you can rest your mind about my safety. I'll call you if he lets me. Take care now. I love you, brother."

He drew her hands to him and kissed them in return. "I'll do all I can to get you out of this mess, Ellie."

"End of conspiracy. Speak English," Douglas ordered. He draped a blanket around Elgiva's shoulders and took her arm. His eyes were shuttered and unhappy; more so after a sound of grief broke from Elgiva's throat without her permission. She ducked her head and struggled for composure.

"You bastard," Rob said to him. "You're breaking her heart, and you don't care."

Douglas ignored him. "Elgiva, you agreed to leave with me. Now keep your word."

"Good-bye, all," she said gruffly.

"Good-bye, your ladyship," John Callum whispered.

"God go with you, Lady Elgiva," Richard Maxwell offered.

"Bless you, cousin," Andrew said hoarsely.

"I apologize for doubting you," Duncan grumbled.

"Ellie," Rob murmured in a torn voice. "Remember, he's only a Kincaid. A MacRoth will never be bested by a Kincaid."

Elgiva swung away, and with Douglas's firm hand guiding her mercilessly, left the cottage.

"You do realize," Audubon asked over a thin, imported cigar, "that you've given Elgiva MacRoth plenty of reasons to despise you? I'm curious as to how you intend to repair the damage."

"She's done some damage of her own." Douglas lifted a hand and stroked his temple. Watching Elgiva suffer tonight had given him a fierce headache. "She's not above manipulating me in ways I don't care to discuss," he added by way of self-defense.

Douglas turned and gazed, frowning, past the plush black couches and teakwood tables of his private jet. Toward the back of the cabin were a set of double doors. Elgiva was asleep—or at least pretending to be asleep—in the bedroom. Sam lay by the door, looking forlorn.

"Sam seems to be on her side," Audubon observed.

"She's brainwashed him with food. She makes herself easy to like." When he faced forward in his seat again, Douglas stared out the window at a night sky as bleak as his mood. "But she's hell on wheels when you make her mad."

"Nice sweater you're wearing," Audubon commented. "Did she knit it for you? In Druradeen her work has quite a reputation for excellence. What a marvelous gift."

"I *earned* it."

"What do you plan to do with her?"

"Overwhelm her. Make her admit that she'd enjoy having what my money could buy for her. Maybe I'll offer to market her sweaters all over the world. Hmmm. Yeah. That's a good idea."

"A strange revenge. And then?"

"She'll admit that she was wrong about me."

"Oh? So you're not going to purchase the MacRoth estate?"

"Of course I am. But I want her to admit that I'm capable of treating it well."

"Will she admit this before or after you evict all of her relatives and friends?"

Douglas groaned. "I'm not going to evict any tenants. My God, it'd be like kicking Andy and Aunt Bee out of a Scottish version of Mayberry. I never realized what the place meant to them."

"A change of heart? How interesting."

"But that's a secret between you and me. Elgiva is going to see things my way first."

"Oh, and *then* you can be chivalrous, when you've humbled her?"

"Dammit, Audubon! I'm not trying to humble her. It's only—" Douglas shoved his hands through his hair. "I don't know how to give up my territory without a fight. I love to negotiate, but in the end I have to be the winner—it's my only obsession. I suppose I developed it when I was a kid. Obsessions put food on the table. Obsessions paid my father's medical bills. And my sister's."

"I understand. But I think you need to conquer this outmoded obsession before it costs you someone about whom you care very deeply."

"I just want to prove to her that she loves me regardless of anything else."

"Did it occur to you that she might love you now?"

"Not after what she did to me a few hours ago." Douglas placed a call from the air-to-ground telephone on a console beside his chair. "Gert? Yes, it's yours truly. Yes, I'm fine. . . . Hmmm. So you were able to keep the family from knowing where I was? . . . They think I've been in Paris? . . . Good work. . . . Yes, I'll give you all the details later. Gert, I'm on my way to the island.

"Have the staff meet me down there within twenty-four hours. And Gert, I have a personal project that needs your attention. First of all, I need a complete wardrobe for a woman who's six feet tall and weighs somewhere in the neighborhood of 'twelve stone.' How much is that in American lingo? . . . Ah-ha. . . . That much, eh? . . . No, every stone is in the right place. Hmmm. Yes. The green dress. She's *that* woman. Now here's what I want . . ."

Twenty minutes later he finished giving his assistant directions for Elgiva's arrival at the Isle of Kincaid. Audubon puffed slowly on his cigar and smiled at him under contemplative, half-shut eyes that were the muted green of old money. "If you're going to keep Elgiva MacRoth, you need to offer a lot more than expensive bribes," he said.

Douglas laughed grimly. "I believe I can manage a *little* personal magnetism."

"Good." Audubon reached into a burnished leather briefcase on the seat beside him and withdrew a folder, which he handed to Douglas. It was full of information on Elgiva. "My friend," Audubon said glibly, "Elgiva MacRoth is made of the finest grade of steel. I hope your magnet is exceptional."

Satin. Blue satin sheets on a king-sized water bed. A *heated* king-sized water bed. In a bedroom the size of her whole apartment over the shop in Druradeen. And this was just the bedroom on Douglas's private plane. She listened sadly to the soft hum of the jets. She didn't even know where Douglas was taking her.

Elgiva lay on one side, fully dressed, her hands huddled against her chest, tears sliding onto the cool satin cover of the pillow as she stared at a stereo system that covered one wall. Behind her she heard the soft click of the room's double doors. Elgiva clamped her eyes shut and nuzzled her tear-streaked face into the pillow, as if she were asleep.

Douglas settled onto the bed close to her back. She smelled the familiar scent of his wool sweater—a scent only a woolens expert would know—but more than that, she knew the scents of his skin and his hair. They were still on her body, still in her soul.

His leg nestled against her as he leaned forward. Elgiva couldn't feign sleep any longer after his big, blunt fingertips touched the tears on her face. Her expression set in careful lines of resistance, she turned over on her back and stared up at him. He looked disgruntled and tired, with grizzled beard stubble on his cheeks. His black hair was badly ruffled. His dark eyes grew more shadowed as he studied her.

"You look like the devil's hind end," she observed in a small voice that came out sounding more distraught than she'd planned.

"So do you." He mumbled a weary curse. "Audubon has a file of information on you," he told her. "I just finished reading it."

"Oh? Sizing up your worst enemy, are you? Tell me what you learned that makes you look like a thundercloud."

"Your grandparents opened MacRoth Hall to the allied forces as a convalescent hospital during the war. They contributed most of their personal savings to the hospital, and they were never reimbursed. By the time your father inherited the place, it was badly run-down. Your father was a struggling poet; your mother was a seamstress. Between them, there wasn't enough money to keep up any kind of estate, much less one the size of theirs."

"Aye. So far you're right. For whatever it means. Home is home, no matter how shabby, and we thought it was a grand place." She was bewildered.

"Along came mean-spirited Uncle Angus, who'd been away for years making himself a fortune in dubious investments. He wanted the estate; his brother wouldn't sell. There was a mysterious fire in the upstairs living quarters. You were nine years old; Rob was seven. Your parents tied bed sheets around you both and lowered you to the ground. But by then it was too late for them to save themselves.

"You saw them burn. You didn't speak a word for two years after that, and Rob stuttered until he was a teenager. Some people said the fire was Angus's doing, but there was no proof. Angus inherited the estate."

He stopped for a moment. His fingers idly stroked a strand of hair from Elgiva's forehead. Whether the action was meant to be soothing or simply to remind her that he was in charge, she couldn't tell. But it felt soothing. "Go on," she murmured.

"He didn't want either you or Rob around. He turned you both out. Gave you to a pair of his crofters—an elderly farmer and his wife—to raise. After they died, the other tenants, including the people in the village, formed a sort of coalition to make certain that the two of you were raised decently. You were shuffled from home to home, with nothing much to call your own."

Elgiva swallowed hard and forced herself to nod. "Aye."

"Jonathan MacMillian loved you and married you, just as his mother and your mother had planned years earlier. His family was convinced that you'd inherit the MacRoth estate someday. After Angus announced that he wasn't leaving *anything* to you or Rob, Jonathan's family accused you of deceiving their simple, good-hearted boy.

"Jonathan never complained about the inheritance, but after he was killed at sea his family made your life miserable. They said that he hadn't cared whether he lived or died—that all the years of a poor, childless marriage had depressed him. They said you married him just to have a home. Finally you gave up your married name out of guilt because you began to believe that they were right, that you *had* ruined him."

Elgiva suddenly understood why Douglas was reciting her history to her. She wanted to scream at the unfairness of it. "So you think I'm a deceptive creature by nature," she said in a tight, vibrating voice, "who'll do anything to get her own way in the world?"

He trailed his fingers down the side of her face. Slowly he cupped her chin. Holding her in that tender grip, he whispered, "No. I also know that you gave up a scholarship at the university in Edinburgh to marry Jonathan. You could have studied art. That was what you'd always wanted to do. But you honored your mother's wishes and married the boy she'd picked for you when you were a child. A boy who'd become a quiet, shy man who loved you regardless of what your uncle would or wouldn't give you someday. You paid a debt of honor."

Elgiva's breath shattered the silence between them. "Mr. Audubon must be very good at investigating people," she said blankly. "I didn't think anyone could find out that much about me. Why are you interested in my history, Douglas?"

He gave her an inscrutable smile. "I want to know what you hold dear. I believe you said the same thing to me, a week or so ago."

"And then?"

He gave her a wicked, though rather shaky, leer. "It's a surprise."

"Where are we going tonight? Where will we end up?"

He rose from the bed. His hand trailed over her lips. "Paradise," he murmured. "Now get some sleep, El."

As he left the room he paused at the ornate double doors to look back at her. She was shocked to see tears in his eyes. They haunted her like a dark promise.

Paradise certainly had a nice airport.

Elgiva gazed out the jet's window at modern buildings, tall palm trees, and blue sky. When Douglas went to shave, Audubon sat down in a chair beside her. "Would you like some advice before I leave you and Douglas alone to do battle?" he asked solemnly. Audubon was returning to his home in America.

"I'd appreciate any words of wisdom."

"Be patient with him. He's not accustomed to making decisions based on sentiment. He doesn't want to look like a fool."

"He'd rather be thought of as heartless?"

"In a way, yes. It's a power position. But I think you understand that it's just an act."

"Sometimes I'm not certain. But I'll keep your advice in mind."

"Good. Because I'd love to see you raise hell with his attitude."

Elgiva smiled dryly. "Rest easy, because I'm very good at *that.*"

A few minutes later she and Douglas left the jet and descended its stairs to the runway. Sam galloped ahead of them, barking his welcome to a tall young man who crossed the tarmac with pantherlike grace.

Douglas stroked the small of her back, startling her even through her heavy sweater. "You're in my prison now," he said. "I hope you have more fun than I had in *your* prison."

Elgiva stared dully at the tropical scenery. "I'll be as troublesome as you were to me."

"Then I'll have to seduce you all over again."

"You won't seduce me as long as you intend to take the MacRoth land."

"Oh, I think I can make you appreciate my point of view."

"You're a cocky devil, I'll give you that."

The air was balmy enough without Douglas's talk about seduction. She felt too warm in her wool clothes. Above her a large commercial jet soared toward the sun, its engines very loud. Elgiva covered her ears and gazed at the man who'd come to greet them.

A glossy black braid hung down his back, somehow looking elegant rather than odd with his crisp dress shirt and tailored white slacks. He clasped Douglas's outstetched hand with apparent warmth and flashed a reserved but genuine smile. When the jet noise died down, Douglas introduced him to her.

His name was Kash Santelli. He spoke English with an odd, pretty accent. Douglas explained that Santelli managed several Kincaid enterprises and also supervised the staff at his private island.

Douglas's island—so that was where they were headed. At least she had a clue now. She searched her memory for things Douglas had said about it. Ah. He'd mentioned his island in the Caribbean. But where in the Caribbean? She recalled the area from her school history lessons only as a tropical place where pirates had once stored their slaves and booty.

Elgiva nodded ruefully to herself. Well, it suited Douglas, then.

He took her arm and guided her toward a helicopter. As he strode along between her and Kash Santelli he reminded Elgiva of a general returning home in victory. A Wall Street general. He and Santelli discussed stock prices and retail indexes in complicated language that made her feel very defensive.

Douglas's ideal woman would be contributing to this conversation instead of stomping along in dumb silence. But then, Elgiva wasn't expected to be ideal. Douglas thought of her as a prisoner, and that only for a short while.

To distract her depressed thoughts she studied Kash Santelli. His features were an exotic mixture—a hooked nose, graceful cheekbones, and large, slanted eyes that hinted at an Oriental influence. Those eyes were black, and his skin was the light umber of Terkleshire honey. He and Douglas called each other by first names. Douglas seemed to like and trust him.

Douglas helped her into the large helicopter emblazoned with "Kincaid" on its side in gold scroll. He steered her to one of a dozen richly upholstered seats, then went forward to greet the pilots. Sam flopped on the floor, panting in the warm weather.

Elgiva watched the pilots talk animatedly with Douglas. His employees seemed to be on very familiar terms with him, though they were also very respectful.

Kash Santelli sat down near her, his face carefully composed but not unfriendly. Elgiva leaned close and whispered, "Could you tell me where we are, lad?"

His black eyes studied her with surprise. In a deep, accented voice he answered solemnly, "St. Thomas. The Virgin Islands."

"And where are we headed?"

"To Douglas's island, about an hour's flight from here."

When Santelli gazed at her with grave speculation, she explained, "I'm here to repay a debt to Mr. Kincaid, you might say. I'm a wee bit in the dark about his plans. Can you tell me what to expect of this island?"

Santelli's eyes flickered with increasing bewilderment. "Well, Ms. MacRoth—"

"Call me Elgiva, lad."

"Elgiva. I don't quite understand this situation. Douglas usually comes here alone or with his immediate family. Occasionally he holds business meetings at the island, but this is the first time he's brought a personal friend."

"You mean he doesn't ferry any little blond women over to keep him company?"

Now somberly amused, Santelli shook his head. Before he could say more, Douglas returned. He gripped Elgiva's shoulder and sat down beside her. "Watch out, Kash. This woman will have you believing that Scottish fairies dance on your ancestors' tombstones."

"*Your* ancestors had no tombstones," Elgiva retorted lightly.

"That's because I have no Scottish ancestors."

"The reivers tossed themselves into Loch Talrigh rather than burn in their own beseiged castle. They fed the fishes."

"Oh. Hatchery workers, hmmm?"

"Phew. The loch must have stunk for years afterward."

In reply to Douglas's exasperated, slit-eyed look she smiled patiently. Over Douglas's shoulder she saw Santelli's startled black eyes. He nodded to her, looking impressed.

Hmmm, perhaps he was like Audubon, and felt that Douglas needed an attitude adjustment. She might have allies here that she'd never expected. And no blondes had preceded her, eh? Elgiva chuckled, earning wary looks from Douglas, as the helicopter left St. Thomas and headed across the vast, blue-green Caribbean sea. No blondes. It was a good sign.

Eight

Dammit, how could she look so unimpressed by a forty-room villa filled with antique wicker, an army of servants, and glorious tropical plants in full bloom? Douglas admired her stone-faced nonchalance at the same time that he cursed it.

She strolled around, nodding as if he were an idiot in need of pacifying as he showed her the magnificent tiled balconies and terraces, all with glorious views of the sea. Her cool amber eyes mocked him by not registering even the slightest bit of awe. He stood among a long wall of French doors in the main salon, his arms spread to the warm, fragrant breeze as he described how the island had once belonged to a pirate.

"Yo ho ho," she intoned dryly.

He felt like a fool.

In the library he showed her a ten-million-dollar painting by a leading Impressionist, an artist his investment brokers had urged him to collect. "Very nice," she commented. "But couldn't you afford a Monet?"

Then she went to his bookcases and scruntinized a few of the titles. "Now here are the *real* interests of Douglas Kincaid," she announced, tapping the books with a fingertip. "Biographies of ruthless men who made a great deal of money."

"Yeah, I'm a real monster," he growled. "Check the psychology books on the other wall. My favorite is *I'm Okay—You're Poor*."

He hauled her to the fifty-person movie theater and pointed out the concession stand outfitted with a wine rack. He took her to the largest of the formal dining rooms so that she could admire a table of glass and burnished wicker that would seat a hundred. He led her down the large hallway that ran the width of the house, hoping to impress her with the rare parrots who squawked hello from their 14-karat gold perches and preened in the sunlight from arched windows set in whitewashed stone.

"Such a pleasant home," Elgiva observed quaintly. "For a man who has no wife or children to keep him good company in it."

"To hell with good company," he shot back. "I have you."

He took her outdoors and drove her around the island in one of the shiny white Jeeps, pointing out the man-made lagoon with its waterfall, the gardens ablaze in tropical color, the clusters of coconuts in the palms along the beach, the guest homes, and assorted private pools.

She expressed enthusiasm only when she saw the goats and cows grazing in pretty pastures on the hillsides. "You need some nice sheep here, Douglas," she noted. "To keep all these jungle plants nibbled down."

Annoyed but amused, he continued on. Douglas guided the Jeep around the base of terraced hills planted in fruit trees. A minute later he parked at the island's tiny bay, where a three-masted sailing yacht and various smaller vessels were anchored at a long dock.

She read aloud the names on their bows. *Kincaid's Prize, Kincaid's Winner, Kincaid's Big Deal, Kincaid's Ace*. Then she turned toward him, squinting innocently in the afternoon sunshine. "Do you intend to stencil your name somewhere on *my* bow?"

"Yes," he retorted. *"Kincaid's Big Mistake."* She chuckled at that.

By the time they returned to the villa he was ready to chew his tongue. "Hot?" he asked with devilish pleasure, watching her tug at the neck of her black wool sweater. Wisps of damp chestnut hair had escaped from her braid and clung to her forehead. She looked flushed and sexy as hell, but he knew she was miserable. He was roasting in his own cold-weather clothes, but he wouldn't admit it.

"A wee bit warm, yes," she acknowledged. She arched a brow. "You didn't let me bring along any clothes. What can I wear now?"

"You'll be naked most of the time, so it won't matter."

She stiffened proudly but her eyes revealed abject concern. "You're not going to make a mockery of the wonderful feelings that happened between us, are you?"

"How would I do that?"

Her gaze held his without teasing or challenge. "By taking me to bed just to be spiteful. Just to prove that I have to do anything you want."

He resisted an urge to draw her into his arms and erase the devastated look from her eyes. Trying hard to remain impassive, he said gruffly, "Whatever happens will be something you want too." With growing dismay he added, "Did you think I was going to lock you in my bedroom and give you orders? Do you think I'm capable of doing that?"

She shook her head. "But you have more subtle ways of getting what you want. A man doesn't have to squeeze the bagpipes hard if he knows how to coax the music from them gently."

Douglas stared at her in droll consternation. "I haven't had much luck up to now. I've gotten a lot of horrible squawks."

She curled her hands around his forearm and

gazed intently into his eyes. "What do you want of me here, Douglas? What am I supposed to do?"

"Stop pretending that you're unfazed by luxury. Relax. Let yourself be pampered. Give *my* life a chance."

She looked shocked. "And then?"

"After I settle the purchase of the MacRoth estate, we'll talk about 'And then.' "

"But you could buy the estate right away, if you wanted. You've only got two weeks left on the option."

"Be pleasant and stop asking questions! That's all I want! No more questions!"

"But—"

"Woman, you'd drive a dog to bite his own tail!"

"You sound very Scottish when you yell like that."

"And not one more damned word about me having Scot ancestors!"

She put her hands on her hips. "Do you always yell at your houseguests? I suppose all your women come here to let you yell at them nonstop."

"Yes. Dozens of women. All blonde. All—"

"Petite. Aye." She smiled crookedly, almost as if she knew something that she wasn't telling.

Douglas groaned in disgust and grabbed her hand again. "Move it, doll. We've got a fashion show to attend."

"A fashion show?" she inquired, as he tugged her down the hall. "But why—"

"No more questions!"

He was going to keep the upper hand in this situation. Somehow. But his control was definitely slipping.

Elgiva glanced down at herself in amusement. She was dressed in a cool white caftan that felt wonderful against her hot skin. A maid in a pink uniform had brought it to her in this beautiful, pastel-colored room. Outside a row of louvered doors was a terrace with a fountain in the center. Beyond the terrace the surf could be heard whooshing against the beach. A tiny monkey chattered on his perch beside a cluster of tall indoor trees.

The maid, a pleasant little woman who spoke with a Spanish accent, had shown Elgiva to an adjacent room and helped her change into the shapeless, flowing caftan. Naked under the strange garment, Elgiva had watched wistfully as the maid had carried her old clothes away. They made her homesick.

But now, sitting in a deep wicker chair with her bare feet propped up on silk-covered pillows, she was almost, well, intrigued. She sipped from a crystal goblet filled with ice and mineral water and topped with an artistically scalloped orange wedge. She looked over at Douglas who had traded his woolens for a white caftan one of his valets had brought.

Only Douglas Kincaid could look utterly masculine in such a strange garment.

He had draped himself along the blue pillows of a wicker lounge. His bare feet—big and handsome, like the rest of him—were crossed at the ankles. He drank from his own goblet of mineral water and sighed with pleasure, running a hand through his disheveled black hair. He made Elgiva think of a contented sheik waiting to be entertained by his harem.

Only he kept watching her as if she were the harem's only member.

"What now?" she asked, then bit her lip. "Oh. Sorry. No more questions."

"Are you comfortable?" She nodded. "Good. As soon as you finish with this little task you can take a shower and soak in your suite's hot tub." He nodded graciously. "You have your own suite of rooms. Right next to mine."

"How thoughtful of you, Douglas. What did you mean by 'This little task'?"

A phone console beeped on the table next to his lounge. He tapped a button. "Yes?"

"Monsieur K, all is ready."

"Fantastic, Gert. Come in and meet Elgiva."

Elgiva straightened politely and pulled her feet to the floor which was inlaid with delicate patterns of light-colored wood. From a hallway entrance marched a compact woman in a white suit with red pinstripes. Her white pumps clicked on the floor. Her brunette hair was cut in a short, fashionably asymmetrical style so that one side swung against her cheek and the other side barely nudged the top of her ear.

Her makeup was perfect and dramatic, and her jewelry consisted of a few very expensive-looking good pieces. She carried a white clipboard, a white notepad, and a gold pen.

She marched up to Elgiva, stopped, and thrust out a hand. "Welcome, Madame. I'm Gert Duval, Monsieur K's executive assistant."

Elgiva returned the handshake. The woman had a mean grip, and for a second Elgiva was tempted to suggest that she visit the pub in Druradeen and arm wrestle with Timothy Kerr, the local champion. Elgiva squeezed back and kept her determined gaze on Gert Duval's haughty one. Slowly, respect began to creep into Gert's eyes.

"I've seen friendlier handshakes between guys who are getting ready to trash each other in the ring," Douglas commented dryly. "Is there a problem here?"

Gert stepped back. "Pardon me, Monsieur. I'm afraid that my loyalty won't let me forget that the lady kidnapped you."

"I appreciate a person with such loyalty," Elgiva told her sincerely. "But you shouldn't condemn me without knowing all my reasons."

"Later," Douglas instructed, sounding impatient. "Gert, she's got reasons. Trust me. Now, have you contacted the staff?"

"Yes. They'll all arrive during the night, Monsieur."

"Good. I'll meet with them tomorrow morning at

ten o'clock. I want updates from everyone. We'll get back to business. But for the moment let's see what you've arranged for my little kidnapper to wear."

"I have everything from lingerie to formal wear, Monsieur. And the selection of jewelry you requested."

"You're incredible, Gert. Thank you."

"It was nothing, Monsieur. I'm just so pleased that you've returned safely."

Elgiva watched Gert Duval settle in a straight-backed chair. As had Kash Santelli, she gave respect without fear, friendship without fawning. If Douglas were the kind of man who deserved such devotion, how could he also be the kind who would take her ancestral home?

She loved him, and she could only hope for the best. But what was he up to now?

He yawned. "All right, Gert, what's first?"

"Swimsuits, Monsieur."

"Hmmm. My favorite, next to lingerie, of course." He motioned to Elgiva, his dark eyes languid and teasing. "Pick out whatever you like, doll. Or take them all."

Gert clapped her hands. A model entered the room wearing the tinest of black bikinis. Elgiva swallowed a knot of embarrassment and shot Douglas a cocky look. "A brownie shrank that swimsuit in the wash. It's bewitched."

"I thought Madame favored this kind of exposure," Gert explained in a proper voice.

Elgiva smiled grimly. "Madame was in costume the night she kidnapped your employer. Madame does not normally show her highlands to the world."

"Next model," Douglas said, repressing a laugh.

The next one wore an even racier bikini—little more than strings and small triangles of red material. Elgiva sighed grandly and tried to ignore the blush rising in her cheeks.

"I cannot wear *that*," she told Douglas. "My poor fair skin would get sunburned in places that I can't even imagine."

"I can," he said cheerfully.

"I must have misjudged Madame's taste," Gert allowed.

Elgiva folded her hands in her lap and looked at Douglas's assistant with calm dignity. "Under the circumstances, I understand your dislike for me. But please give me a chance to make my reputation on more than one night's appearance."

Gert looked perplexed. "Perhaps you'll like the next selection."

The third model wore a simple maillot of shimmering blue material. Although it was the kind of suit that clung to every curve, it was demure compared to the others. Elgiva nodded fervently. "That will do!"

Gert gazed at her with growing curiosity. "It comes in five different colors."

"Get her one of each," Douglas interjected.

Elgiva took a convulsive swallow of the iced mineral water and tried not to gape at him. He studied her face, and a slow, victorious smile slid across his mouth. "It can be fun to be rich," he murmured. "It can make you reassess your whole outlook."

So that was his goal. To win her loyalty with bribes. Elgiva's hands tightened harshly on her goblet. If he loved her he would already know that bribes weren't necessary, and that they couldn't make her happy if he still planned to buy the MacRoth estate.

"I don't need to see anymore," she said abruptly, standing up. "This won't do you any good, Douglas. Keep your bribes."

"They're not bribes," he said, but he looked startled. He propped his arms on his knees and sat forward, scrutinizing her like a playful sultan who'd suddenly had his top concubine spit in his eye.

"Was that to be your revenge?" she asked. "To buy my change of heart and then gloat because you'd proved your golden rule—that everybody has a price?"

He didn't answer immediately, but a fleeting look

of guilt swept across his expression. It was true, then, Elgiva thought sadly. "It won't work," she said in a low, anguished voice. "I've already given you the results you wanted in your experiment with loneliness, and now you'd like to see if I'm greedy, as well. No."

His face tightened into a mask of reserve. "Not greedy. Realistic."

She looked at Gert, who was frowning thoughtfully at her boss. "Can you show me to my suite?" Elgiva asked her.

Douglas scowled. Gert shifted awkwardly. "Monsieur K?"

"All right. Go on, for now." Tension radiated from the tightly held lines of his body as he gazed at Elgiva. "I'll have the maids bring this whole wardrobe to your suite. You can either wear it or go naked. I don't care."

"You don't care about anyone's pride but your own," Elgiva said softly, her throat tight with tears of disappointment. "You can only give when it suits your purposes, Douglas, and that's not what giving is supposed to be about."

She left the room with Gert hurrying after her. Elgiva heard the crash of crystal and pictured Douglas slamming his goblet against the floor.

"My, he's never done *that* before," Gert noted in a taut little voice. She hesitated, then added as if talking to herself, "Maybe it was time. Maybe, indeed, you are right, Madame."

"Call me Elgiva."

"Call me Gert. And tell me how you know Monsieur K so well."

Elgiva stopped. Around her in the luxurious hallway parrots chattered and tropical plants reached out with beautiful blossoms, promising a world as perfect and unreal as anything a fairy ever ruled.

"I understand him because he needs his legends the way I need mine," she told Gert with a shaky,

;ardonic smile. "It will be interesting to see whose egends survive."

"How long have you known Douglas?" Elgiva asked Kash Santelli. He paused over his glass of juice and studied her across a patio table set with china and silver. He had come to ask if her breakfast was satisfactory.

She suspected that he'd agreed to sit down because he felt sorry for her. After a sleepless night, Elgiva knew that even a Paris sundress and a maid's skillful attention to her hair couldn't make her look less than woeful.

"I have worked for him since I graduated from Harvard, and that was six years ago," the exotic-looking young man replied finally, his accent making music with the words. "Before that, well, I lived at Audubon's estate in Virginia from the time I was ten, so I saw Douglas on many occasions over the years. You could say that I've known him most of my life."

When she tried to restrain her curiosity he smiled, though his black eyes never lost their guarded look. She suspected that they never did. "When I was ten, Douglas and Audubon rescued me from a brothel in Vietnam," Kash told her. "They were in the American army at the time."

"Oh, I see." Elgiva ducked her head and idly pushed a heavy, sterling silver fork into a plate filled with sliced fruit. She tried to contain her shock and dismay. *A brothel. Douglas had gone to a brothel.*

"He and Audubon were only looking for a friend of theirs," Kash said.

She jerked her head up and found him watching her knowingly. Elgiva sighed and tossed her fork onto the plate. "You must think I'm a naive person. I didn't mean to look as if the idea startled me."

"Why not? It *disgusts* me. I'm disgusted by the

idea of people being forced to sell themselves and their children." At her stunned reaction he nodded calmly. "My mother died shortly after I was born. She was a prostitute. Half Vietnamese and Egyptian." He laughed ruefully. "The story behind *that* interesting combination will have to wait for another time." His mouth tightened. "My father was an American—not a soldier, obviously, since I was already ten years old at the time of the war, but an American, nonetheless. Douglas and Audubon felt sorry for me, I suppose. They smuggled me out of Vietnam."

"So you had been raised in the brothel," Elgiva ventured, her stomach twisting with sympathy and dread.

His dark eyes held hers without flinching. "Yes. And I *worked* in the brothel. There are many sad fates for children in a poor country, Elgiva. Especially for handsome little boys."

Elgiva raised a glass of water to her lips and took a deep swallow, fighting for calm. She failed. Thumping the glass down, she grasped one of Kash's hands. "I despise people who harm children! I'm so sorry for you! I hope you find a great deal of happiness to erase the terrible memories. I hope you have a ladyfiend who loves you and understands."

He looked startled by her outburst. "Well, I have several who understand. I don't think I'd say that *love* is uppermost in their minds, however."

Elgiva pulled her hand away and blushed. "Och! I've been incredibly personal and nosy. Forgive me."

But his eyes gleamed with affection. "Now I understand why Douglas considers you so special," he said softly. "You are truly a kind and caring person."

"But I didn't mean to embarrass you."

"You didn't. Besides, no one can tell when I blush." His eyes twinkled as he pointed to his honey-colored complexion. "An asset. For the record, my full name is James Kashadlan Yung Santelli. Multicultural, wouldn't you say? A Vietnamese-Egyptian mother from Saigon and an Italian-American father from New Jersey."

Elgiva buried her forehead in both hands and propped her elbows on the table. The threads of Douglas's life were unique in ways she had never suspected. "So Douglas and Audubon saw to it that you had a good life in America?"

"Yes. Douglas paid for my education at Harvard. Audubon was a wonderful adopted father, but he had no immediate family. For family, I had the Kincaids. They gave me a feeling of kinship."

Elgiva chuckled dryly. "Then consider yourself Scottish too."

"Excuse me?"

"It's a little argument between myself and Douglas. Never mind." She pulled a linen napkin from her lap and wound it around her fingers in a gesture that was both distracted and tense. "What was Douglas like many years ago, before he became successful?"

"Much like he is today. Driven. Dramatic. Full of energy and plans. Able to bring out the best in people while at the same time charming them into doing exactly what he wanted. He needed all of that to survive in the business world. After he returned to Chicago from the army he took his small savings and bought a grocery store in a very bad section of town.

"He fought street gangs, drug pushers, and every other kind of ugly type you can imagine, but he kept that grocery running. He even made it profitable. Gradually he bought and renovated other buildings on the same street. In five years' time he turned a slum neighborhood into a safe, clean place to live. And he made a lot of money in the process."

Kash paused. "You have to understand that most of Douglas's projects serve such dual purposes. He makes a profit, certainly, but he makes improvements, as well."

Elgiva stared at him, feeling troubled and confused. "Do you know anything about the nursing home he bought a few years ago? The one he demolished to build a parking lot? There were such ugly insinuations about him in the American newspapers. Several of the residents died from the grief of moving."

Kash nodded. "The home was a disgrace. Elderly people were suffering there. It's true that Douglas wanted the site, but it's also true that many years earlier his father had died in that home from an overdose of medication given by a drunken orderly. His father was paralyzed from a boxing injury when Douglas was only a child, you see."

"I knew about his father's injury." Elgiva pressed a hand to her throat. "But I didn't know that he died in a terrible way."

"From what Douglas has told me—and it's something he rarely discusses—his father became too incapacitated to remain at home. The family had no idea, of course, that they were placing him in a nursing facility that was poorly run."

"So years later, Douglas bought it and shut it down."

"Yes. And he moved the residents to a much nicer place. The stress of the transfer was something no one could have foreseen. Douglas was horrified by what happened."

"But he didn't defend himself."

"No, not when it would mean discussing his father. He's a very private man where his family is concerned."

"And where his personal life is concerned." She studied the vista of sea and gardens and, on the hillsides beyond the main estate, the red-tiled roofs of small guest houses peeking out of the forest. He would buy the MacRoth land and turn it into a Scottish version of this paradise. He would have to have his privacy there, as he did here. He wasn't a cruel man, just one who had never been able to indulge in too much trust.

"You have brought something new to his life," Kash commented, his tone thoughtful. "He wants to change his life, perhaps." He looked at a slender gold watch on his wrist. "But for now, he's about to begin one of his marathon business meetings. I must go." He stood. "I doubt you'll see Douglas again before tomorrow. He has a lot of business to catch up with due to his unusual and, might I add, much-needed vacation recently."

Elgiva smiled through a mist of tears. "Thank you, Kash. I'll be fine. Thank you for everything."

He touched her shoulder. "The moments of revelation in life are sometimes small and unnoticed at first. Have patience."

He left her there alone in the beautiful morning, her mind filled with thoughts of Douglas, the mystifying man whom she loved more than ever.

After two days of nonstop meetings and dozens of phone calls, Douglas felt that he had regained command of his far-flung business deals, including the option on the MacRoth estate. Nettled by his new intentions for compromise, Douglas postponed a decision on its purchase.

He was anxious to spend time with Elgiva, if only to hear her melodic, charming voice raised in some insult to his past, present, and future. Since he'd had people reporting to him about every step she took and every word she said, he quickly learned that she was reading a book beside the lagoon.

Douglas followed a footpath through the lush gardens, brushing aside vines heavy with purple blossoms and palm fronds that rattled against his khaki slacks and white golf shirt. He was going to take time to actually *play* golf as soon as he built a golf course beside MacRoth Hall.

The man-made lagoon resembled something out of a Hollywood fantasy, with lovely, draping trees around the perimeter. At one end a waterfall tumbled over pearl-gray rocks. He caught his breath as he saw Elgiva sitting on the edge of a boulder that jutted over the water, a dozen feet below.

Her hair was a tapestry of beautiful reds and golds held back from her face by jade combs. She wore jade-green shorts that were pleated and loose, like a skirt. With them she wore a white tube top and white sandals. Elgiva in a tube top and shorts. He stopped to admire that incredibly provocative view.

She looked up from her book and froze when she saw him. Slowly she shut the cover, her hands settling atop it with a calculated nonchalance that alerted his suspicions.

"Contemplating some new legends?" he inquired in a jaunty tone as he went to her and dropped to his haunches. The mild taunt was lost as his gaze met hers; the elemental welcome in her eyes held him spellbound. In that second he was tempted to toss her book aside and coax her back on the warm, smooth rock. He sensed that he could succeed easily.

Her face flushed and she chuckled. "This is a lovely spot, Douglas." She pointed to a long rope that hung over the lagoon's center from a massive tree limb. "Do you come here to pretend that you're Tarzan?"

He smiled. "When I was a kid I used to visit a farm owned by my best friend's grandparents. They had a pond with a rope swing over it. I loved it."

"So you're recreating your childhood, are you?"

"Always, doll. With bigger and better toys than I ever knew existed." He touched her cheek and watched in delight as her eyes flickered with barely contained response. "You're looking magnificent. Luxury agrees with you."

"I have to admit, I like having a hot tub on the balcony outside my bedroom. And I like having a massage every morning. And the food your chef serves is *very* good. And these clothes—" she sighed and glanced down at herself—"they're not so bad."

He stroked the backs of his fingers along her jaw. "Is this the same woman who stormed out of the room two days ago after she accused me of trying to bribe her affections?"

Elgiva shrugged. "I was tired and a wee bit on edge from all that had happened in the day or so before that." She looked him over happily, making shivers run down his spine. "You're done with your meetings?"

"Yes. Miss me?"

"I did. I admit it."

Douglas smiled. He'd been overanxious about her stubborn pride. He'd have her in his bed by tonight, and from then on everything would be perfect between them.

He stood and extended a hand. "Why don't we go back to the house for cocktails and a little caviar? Afterward we can have dinner together. Followed by a late night cruise on the yacht."

"I'd love that, Douglas. I truly would."

Cradling her book, she took his hand and stood. Then she brought his palm to her lips and kissed it. He grinned down at her, feeling almost giddy with relief.

"Ah, El. This is going to be great." Abruptly he slid his arms under her and picked her up.

The unexpected action made her lose her grip on the book. It flopped into her lap. Douglas stared at the cover. *Sweet Talk—The Art of Manipulating People Through Sexual Innuendo.*

"Oh, dear," she said in a tiny voice.

He glared at her. "Dammit. Damn it to hell."

"This book came from *your* library."

"I never read this book. It was a gift. Why don't you tell me what else you learned from it? Were we going to play bed games later so that you could try to trap me again?"

She shook her head and her eyes filled with sorrow. But her expression was obstinate. "Put me down, you oaf. I was just trying to fight fire with fire. It shouldn't surprise you."

"Fight fire with water, doll." He stepped to the edge of the boulder and tossed her into the lagoon. His anger gave the toss an adrenaline boost, and she sailed to the center before she splashed down.

Flailing, she grabbed the end of the rope and clung to it. She swiped her hair back and gazed up at him wide-eyed. Douglas crossed his arms over his chest. "Apologize," he ordered curtly.

It was a wonder that the water didn't sizzle around her. She pounded the surface with one hand and jerked on the rope with the other. A long stream of Gaelic careened from her lips, and he knew it wasn't an apology.

"I'll be waiting at the house when you're ready to say that you're sorry," he announced.

"Go on! And hold your breath until I do!"

"Bye, doll."

He walked back to the house, sequestered himself to his private suite, and paced its wide balcony with his eyes trained on the gardens below. An hour later she still had not returned.

Disgusted and depressed, Douglas went to his theater and put an old gangster film in the projector. Then he slumped in a back row seat and shut his eyes. As far as Elgiva was concerned, he was still public enemy number one.

From her place in the center of the lagoon, Elgiva watched the sun sink. She uttered a fierce stream of oaths but heard the fear in her voice. Shivering, she looked nervously at the deep pool and turbulent waterfall. Her gaze searched the dense forest around the tops of the rock walls. This place was too secluded; it looked eerie in the long, empty shadows.

Back home, old people would say that trolls lurked in a place like this at night, or that slimy green kelpies with horrible teeth would—no, no, no, she wasn't going to scare herself with such silliness.

She looked down. The end of the rope floated in the water around her. Elgiva looped it under her armpits and made a crude sling, so that she could let both arms rest. One of the servants would come by eventually, in the morning, perhaps. She'd call for help. If the trolls hadn't gotten her by then.

Elgiva groaned at her own pride. She'd rather be eaten by trolls than tell Douglas that she couldn't swim.

Nine

Douglas believed that a bedroom should be a haven of private pleasures. He never let work intrude there; he banned the fax machines, the computers, the televisions scrolling stock data and interest rates.

The furniture in his bedroom at the villa was sleek and simple; black lacquer and smoked glass, expensive and elegant. Bookcases overflowed with board games, trivia books, and volumes of crossword puzzles. In a room off the master bedroom were a billiard table, a dart board, video games and a giant television screen surrounded by plush couches. A separate room contained a complete professional gym, and through another door was a gourmet kitchen.

In the center of the master bedroom, underneath an abstract painting of muted, relaxing colors, was a giant water bed covered in black silk sheets and a satin bedspread of stark black patterns on a white background. On a floor of gleaming black marble were white rugs so deep that Sam's big paws disappeared in them whenever he padded across.

Douglas sat in the middle of his bed, a black silk robe tied loosely around himself, and scowled wearily at the sterling silver clock on a dresser across the room. It chimed eleven times. Elgiva was probably asleep in her suite by now, dreaming of new ways to aggravate him.

Unable to be still a second longer, Douglas got up and opened all the glass doors along one wall of his suite. The night breezes flooded in, bringing heady scents of the ocean and the gardens. He paced the enormous balcony outside, crisscrossing it in long, angry strides, his shadow chasing him in the light of a full moon.

To hell with indecision. He was going to put his attorneys to work on the MacRoth acquisition. Tomorrow. Elgiva could stop hoping for a compromise. They'd confront each other with the stark reality of the situation; he would own the estate, and if she wanted to be a part of it she'd have to give up her schemes and see things his way.

How could she have run the damned estate, anyway? She and her brother had no money; all the sentimentality in the world couldn't keep the roof of the manor hall from leaking or renovate rooms that had needed the work twenty years ago. What would she dislike worse: Turning the estate over to him, who'd take care of it, or watching the whole place crumble around her?

He muttered to himself darkly. No more procrastination. With this nonsense about her heritage out of the way, she'd settle down. He was going to make a success of this relationship the only way he knew how—by taking charge.

Indoors, a bell rang softly. Douglas went to an intercom and flicked the switch. "Yeah?"

It was Kash. "Gert and I need to see you. It's important." Kash's voice was harsh with restraint.

"Come to my suite."

Douglas slipped into black pajama bottoms and tightened his robe. A minute later he opened the suite's imposing black doors and let his two longtime assistants into the room. Gert, wearing a severe shirtwaist dress, frowned at him. Kash, dressed in white slacks and a white pullover, looked rumpled and angry. His onyx hair was unbraided and hung about his shoulders in damp, disheveled strands.

Douglas studied the two of them worriedly. "What's wrong?"

Kash spoke first. "We never expected you to let your personal frustrations turn into petty revenge. It's not your style, Douglas, and we don't like it."

Gert's arms were rigid by her sides, the hands clenched into fists. "What you did was truly disappointing, Monsieur K. I know that Elgiva MacRoth has caused you difficulties, but I've also seen how obstinate you've been with her. I've talked to her a great deal over the past two days, and I've seen her side of the issues. You are wrong to covet her estate, Monsieur." Gert quivered with restraint, but her voice rose. "And you are despicable for leaving her in the lagoon when you *know* she can't swim!"

A sick feeling of horror rose in Douglas's throat. "*What*? She can't swim?" He grabbed Gert's arm. "Is she all right? Where is she?"

Gert and Kash traded looks of astonishment. "In her suite," Kash said quickly. "She's not hurt. I discovered her at the lagoon when I took a walk before bedtime."

Douglas was already on his way to the door. Gert and Kash caught up with him and blocked his way. "She's asleep," Gert said. "Please, Monsieur, she was upset and tired. Please don't upset her anymore tonight. She's perfectly all right. I called the clinic and had Nina send up a mild tranquilizer to relax her. She's asleep. Please."

Douglas stared at Gert and Kash. "You found her in the lagoon hanging onto the rope?"

Kash nodded. "She had tied it around herself. Other than having muscle cramps from being in the cool water so long, she was fine."

"She could have drowned. My God, she could have drowned. Why didn't she tell me?" He jammed his hands through his hair. "I didn't know. Did she say that I knew she couldn't swim when I left her there?"

"She told me that she fell into the water accidentally," Kash said, his expression somber. "But I sensed that there was something else. She's not very good at concealing the truth. One of the security guards helped me bring her back to the house. He mentioned that he had seen you coming back from the lagoon late this afternoon. I noticed something secretive in Elgiva's eyes that worried me. Finally I got her to admit that you'd thrown her into the water."

Douglas went to a chair and sank down. *I could have killed her,* he thought weakly. "She said that I knew she couldn't swim?"

Gert cleared her throat awkwardly. "No. She said that you weren't to blame, but beyond that she wouldn't discuss the incident. We drew our own conclusions."

"The lady is not one to reveal her humiliation to strangers," Kash explained. "I apologize if Gert and I overreacted, but from what we've learned of Elgiva, we decided that she was the kind of lady who would protect your honor. She was very despondent, and she specifically requested that you not be told about this incident. We, however, felt that we couldn't let it pass."

Gert winced. "I suppose we have meddled too much, Monsieur K. I apologize for doubting you."

"Yes," Kash agreed.

Douglas shook his head. "Don't apologize. I nearly killed her. My God, what kind of tyrant have I become? What stupid pride. I provoked her. She could have told me that she didn't know how to swim, but I made it difficult for her to admit she needed help."

"She's all right," Gert repeated, her voice soothing. "In the morning you can tell her how badly you regret the incident. But please don't try to see her tonight. It will only make matters worse."

"She could have drowned." Douglas put his head in his hands. "Thank you for telling me about this. Now please go. I've got some thinking to do."

Kash touched his shoulder in a silent gesture of

support, then he and Gert left the room. Douglas numbly walked outside and stood in the moonlight, straining his eyes toward Elgiva's balcony. Emotions tore through him until his knees turned to rubber and he had to grasp a railing for support.

He now realized with blinding certainty that he would rather die himself than have anything happen to her.

Elgiva stirred slowly, her thoughts fuzzy from the pill Gert had given her. She blinked, frowned in the darkness of her room, and couldn't decide what had caused her to wake up. She fumbled with the cool silk sheets and tugged vaguely at the low-cut bodice of her nightgown. Glancing at a clock on the wicker nightstand, she saw that she had been asleep for several hours.

Stretching her legs, she felt a foot connect with something large. Something on the corner of her bed. Elgiva raised up on her elbows and squinted frantically. "Douglas!"

He got up, staggered a little, moved forward, and sat down carefully beside her. Even her groggy senses couldn't miss the potent scent of whisky as he leaned over her and braced an arm on the mattress. "You've had a bit too much to drink," she said. "Or is that an understatement?"

He chuckled. "You bet. I'm three plaid sheets to the wind, doll. Go ahead and laugh at me. This doesn't happen very often."

Elgiva groaned softly. People had a tendency to reveal their inner selves when they were in this condition. Jonathan had bellowed at her. Rob became comically sentimental. And on the few occasions when she'd had too much to drink, Elgiva had cried and felt lonely.

She held her breath. What would Douglas do?

His intense, harshly shadowed face was too close for comfort, and her spine tingled at his emotion-filled silence. Trembling, Elgiva lay back. She searched for the right words. "Why are you drinking?" she asked as calmly as she could. "What has upset you?"

"You could have drowned." His slurred voice was anguished and incredibly gentle. "I nearly killed you."

Elgiva was speechless for a moment. "No one was supposed to tell you. I held on to the rope and no harm came to me. My stubbornness wouldn't let me admit to you that I couldn't swim. What happened wasn't your fault."

"Yes, it was. I forced you to fight. It was all my fault." His husky, sorrowful words made her stare at him in amazement. If this was the real Douglas Kincaid, she had cruelly misjudged him before.

"El, I'm so sorry." He cupped her face with one hand and kissed her lightly on the forehead. He was trembling as much as she was, Elgiva discovered. He rested his cheek against her hair. She felt the anguished rise and fall of his chest.

Confusion muddled her already stunned mind. Affection and tenderness grew inside her. "Oh, dear man," she whispered brokenly. "What are you doing to me?"

"Trying to ask you to forgive me." He stroked her hair with a gentle, endearingly clumsy hand. "Please forgive me. I would never have left you in the lagoon if I'd known that you couldn't swim."

Elgiva placed her fingertips against his mouth. "Don't you think I knew that at the time? Of course I forgive you." Tears burned her eyes. "You can't understand why I won't stop fighting you, and I can't understand why you have to have control."

Her burr became thicker, her voice a hoarse, pleading rasp. "Faith, Douglas, you and I willna ever compromise. Go ahead and buy the estate and then let me go. I canna be with you like this. It's tearing me apart."

He took her in his arms and buried his face in the crook of her neck. Elgiva cried out at the undisguised torment in him. This was not the Douglas Kincaid who prided himself on control. Her hands shaking, she slid them up and down his back in a comforting gesture.

"The estate is yours. I won't buy it," he murmured thickly. "I swear."

She gasped and began to cry. "Dear man, please don't say that if it's not true. Oh, Douglas." She stroked him with desperate little movements of her hands.

His arms tightened around her convulsively. "I swear it," he promised. "I want you and your brother to have what should have been yours. I know how much it means to you, how much the people who live there mean to you. I've just been too damned stubborn to admit that sometimes sentiment is all that's important."

"Oh, Douglas." She struggled to put a bit of space between them, his fervent embrace making her breathless, and wound her hands under his chin. Gently she lifted his head. Her mind whirling with impossible hopes, she kissed him deeply.

She pushed his robe from his shoulders and caressed the bared skin of his powerful shoulders and back. Slowly he moved the covers away from her. He got on his knees and pulled her nightgown down gracefully. "Wouldn't want to tear it," he noted quaintly.

Elgiva laughed in broken, giddy delight, tears streaming from the corners of her eyes as he pressed her to the bed and kissed her body, drawing excitement through her veins with each slow, tantalizing movement.

Her hands found the smooth silk of the pajamas covering his legs and gloried in the hard, tightly packed muscle underneath. He made erotic, half-growling sounds in the back of his throat, but they were also gentle. When he parted her thighs and gave her the same uninhibited loving that he'd given once before, she sank her hands into his hair and tossed helplessly, wanting the sensations to go on forever.

"El," he whispered raggedly, as his hands coaxed even more response from her. Her moans brought him to her hurriedly, and she stripped the pajamas down his thighs. Every move he made was laced with vibrant emotion; his hands never stopped roaming over her, and when he thrust into her, his caring touch had made her ready.

Later they lay in a silent, sweet trance, his body heavy and possessive atop hers. The love she felt was rich and full and able to daydream about a future with him.

She kissed his neck as he gathered her hair into a soft pillow for his head. His breath was warm and contented on her shoulder; he began to taste her skin with small flicks of his tongue, making her shiver in delight.

He and she kissed slowly, with great tenderness. Her breath feathering in her lungs, Elgiva floated from sensation to sensation, loving the taste of his mouth, flavored with good Casner's Scotch.

When they stopped kissing and looked at each other, they both smiled. "You're glowing in the dark," he murmured.

"Aye. So are you."

"Are you sure you're all right after what happened at the lagoon?"

"Aye. Just a little waterlogged."

"How about taking a swim in a safer—and smaller— body of water?"

"Well, if you're there with me, certainly."

He began to laugh under his breath, sounding very happy. Charmed and curious, Elgiva caressed him with greedy hands.

"Stop, you insatiable fairy," he whispered. "Come with me." Standing, he wavered, grabbed both her hands in joyful and reckless abandon, and tugged. She bounced out of bed and hugged him, snuggling her belly against his already reviving arousal.

He chortled and led her outdoors into the moonlight. The Jacuzzi waited there, and she yipped when he picked her up and placed her in the tepid, still water. He switched on the heater and jets, then climbed in beside her.

The combination of the sultry night and Douglas's warm body soon made the heater seem unnecessary. With the water bubbling against her below and Douglas kissing her above—not to mention what his hands were doing—she unwound completely.

She had never known such hypnotic pleasure existed; such perfect harmony inside herself because love and desire spiraled together. And the suggestions he was murmuring to her! Even the thought of them was wildly exciting. He didn't know that he was offering exotic candies to a woman who'd never even sampled sugar. She heard her voice answering him through a haze of passion. *Could we? Would you? I'd love to.*

The moon moved across the sky. The night birds stopped singing to listen to the soft symphony of masculine and feminine moans that floated from the balcony. The darkness grew deeper, more private.

Before she fell blissfully asleep with her head pillowed on Douglas's shoulder, laying beside him on the mattress he'd dragged outside in a particularly inspired moment, Elgiva smiled to herself.

Douglas Kincaid had proved himself worthy of legends.

Elgiva kept very still in the swimming pool, glad to feel its pretty blue tiles securely beneath her feet. She smiled down at Douglas, who was floating on his back with his head in her arms. His eyes were well shaded from the sun by her bare breasts.

"I hope you're right about this technique curing your hangover," she said drolly.

He chuckled, the sound muffled against the underside of one breast. "If nothing else, it makes recovery a helluva lot of fun."

He nuzzled the sensitive skin with his lips, and Elgiva sighed in delight. The world was full of vibrant sensations; she was surrounded and filled by ethereal beauty. Shade trees drooped across the pool's rustic stone apron. They dappled sunlight over the white lounge chairs and the swimsuits she and Douglas had discarded soon after they were alone inside the tall, whitewashed walls of the enclosure.

This was Douglas's private area, completely sequestered, with a breezy little cabana of pearl-gray stone at one end. They'd eaten lunch there, sitting close together at a beautiful table the servants had set up before their arrival. Eating lunch naked had been another new experience for Elgiva. Especially dessert.

She stroked a hand across Douglas's chest and admired his body with glowing approval. Given the opportunity, he was as expert as relaxing as he was at mastering other skills. His muscular arms floated peacefully by his sides and his legs rode the crystal-blue water like graceful, though hairy, schooners.

He was tantalizing her deliberately, she was certain, by letting his legs drift apart. She loved his bawdiness, and she had fun admiring him. The parts below the waterline were handsome, but the parts above were awe inspiring.

"I like the islands you make," she told him. She could feel him smiling against her breasts. "Oh, my. Look what my kind words have done. I believe *one* island is having a slight earthquake."

"That island is a volcano."

"Dangerous?"

"You might look at it that way."

"Perhaps I should take a *closer* look." Sliding her hands under him, she kept his body still as she moved down his side. It was thrilling to think about the intimacies she wanted to share with him. It was also worrisome.

He'd given her a great deal of unselfish attention last night and this morning; he'd taken the initiative in his gentle, confident way. She worried that he might discover her naiveté if she didn't make some bold moves in return. How could she keep him if she weren't as sophisticated as his petite, blond candidates for wifehood?

She didn't quite know how to announce her intentions. *Douglas, I want to capture your Loch Ness monster?* No, that wouldn't do. Elgiva shut her eyes and blurted, "I think I'd better do something to please the angry volcano spirits."

"Oh, El." His voice was thick with anticipation. "You're a terrific mind reader."

So he *had* been wondering when she'd do more than just ogle him with adoring eyes. Elgiva nodded to herself. When she wanted to learn a new style of weaving or knitting, she simply attacked it with fervent enthusiasm.

So that was how she attacked Douglas now.

He gave a garbled yelp of pain and surprise, then lurched upright in the water. Elgiva lost her balance and fell over. Quickly he pulled her back. Coughing and sputtering, she stared at his grim expression.

"That wasn't funny, El. I thought we were making love, not playing stupid pranks."

She was beyond embarrassment. She wanted to evaporate. "I didn't mean to hurt you. I'm sorry." Further explanations stuck inside her throat. The humiliation was too great. She turned away quickly and splashed water on her superheated face. Her body felt rigid, as if it had become a shield.

"What made you think I'd like to be gnawed like an ear of corn?" he asked, sounding puzzled and exasperated.

"I'm very sorry. I won't do it again, I promise."

"Why did you do it in the first place?"

She cupped water to her face, washing away tears of angry self-defense. How could she have known what to do? She'd never had a chance to learn!

"I said I'm sorry, Douglas. Could you just be quiet about it?" She heard the sorrowful tremor in her voice and swallowed hard. "Damn."

Suddenly he moved close behind her. His hands clasped her shoulders, squeezing firmly but gently. "I think you need to explain to me," he murmured, and his voice was now soothing. "I have plenty of suspicions anyway. So you might as well confirm them."

She groaned in dismay. "Och! I thought I was doing so well! I should have just taped a great huge sign on my forehead! 'Beware! Bad Lover!' "

"El, El, sssh," he chastised softly. His hands slid back and forth. "You're wonderful. But I realized even when we were in Scotland that you've got more enthusiasm than know-how."

"Aye," she said bitterly, nodding. "And the lack is more obvious than I thought."

"There's only one reason why a sexy, loving woman would feel awkward after twelve years of marriage." He put his arms around her and rested his cheek against the back of her head. "Jonathan must not have given you much opportunity to practice."

Her shoulders slumped. "I don't want to speak ill of him. He was good to me in so many ways."

"This will be our secret, El. I don't want to gossip about Jonathan's faults; I'm just trying to understand you and help you feel better." He turned her around and pulled her head to his shoulder. With his arms around her snugly he whispered, "You're fantastic, El. What you don't know I can teach you. I've never been happier or more satisfied. I hope you feel the same way."

"Oh, yes," she nearly moaned, the words inadequate. "But I can't keep on upsetting you with my mistakes."

He squeezed her in mild rebuke. "No pain, no gain, I always say. And I *love* a challenge."

Elgiva chuckled wearily. "You could end up with permanent scars on your volcano."

"There's a lot more to me than Mount Vesuvius."

"I know, dear man, but I want to be good to every part of you."

He kissed her. Elgiva hugged him and said with painful slowness, "I'll tell you what I was used to, Douglas. I'll tell you." She looked away from the bittersweet compassion in his eyes, struggling to keep her voice casual. "On our wedding night Jonathan said to me, 'Ellie, be still, now. This will just take a minute.' And . . . that's all it took."

"Oh, El."

"And that was more or less his attitude for the next dozen years. He'd say, 'Ellie, pull your gown up, would you?' Or 'Ellie, I've got a little problem that's keeping me awake.' Those were his ways of politely asking permission. I suppose they give you a pretty accurate picture of what followed afterward."

"Yes. Sweet doll, I'm sorry," Douglas whispered. He shook his head. His dark eyes were remorseful. "You went from polite sex with a mild-mannered husband to being leered at by a wild-tempered stranger. No wonder you were threatened by me up in Scotland."

"Not threatened. Overwhelmed. There were times when I thought the bars of your cell were going to melt from the look in your eyes when you watched me. But before long I was *begging* them to melt."

Douglas trailed his fingers down her back, then cupped her rump in his hands. He lifted her against him. She chuckled at the exaggerated lechery in his arched brows and wicked expression.

He carried her into shallower water. "Listen to your professor, you big bonnie lass, and you'll learn everything you always wanted to know. First I'll teach you to tame the volcano. Next I'll teach you to swim."

"Swim? What does that have to do with making love?"

He winked at her. "It all depends on how you learn to stroke."

"Faith!" she exclaimed softly, and kissed him.

. . .

The little things made him love her more. Her guilt-free enjoyment of food. The cozy way she shared his toothbrush and scratched his back and purred like a big, happy cat when he painted her toenails. The fact that she didn't pretend to understand high finance but wasn't shy about telling him her ideas about running a small business.

He loved her for the cutthroat way she played Monopoly. She built up the block around Park Place and gleefully charged him exorbitant rents when he landed there. He loved her for her refusal to feel sorry for herself because she'd missed out on attending college. He loved her for being proud of what she was, and for knowing what she was, and for knowing what she wanted from life.

Unfortunately, what she wanted was to go back to Scotland.

It wasn't that she said anything specific; it was the way she talked about her apartment, and her shop, and the village, and MacRoth Hall, which she was anxious to see now that it was definitely going to belong to her and her brother.

Douglas wondered how difficult it would be to coax her into living elsewhere in the world. He wanted to talk about the future, but he forced himself to wait. Her new trust was too fragile; he'd give her time to believe in him without any misgivings. After all she'd suffered in her marriage, he was afraid that she'd balk at any mention of commitment. For the first time in his life, he was content, and complete, and patient.

And afraid that he was going to lose her because of it.

When they woke up the next morning they were, as usual, halfway to making love. It was fantastic to feel her sleepy mouth nuzzling his and her body already responding to his hands.

Afterward, she lay on top of him with her knees hugging his sides and her arms wound under his neck. "Very *instrrructive*," she cooed. Her accent always deepened when she was happy.

Douglas kissed the tip of her nose. "How would you like to leave for London in a couple of hours?"

"Just like that? You make it sound like a jaunt to the village store."

"It is. We'll take the helicopter over to St. Thomas, then climb aboard my jet. We'll watch a few movies, eat some wonderful food, take a nap, and *voilà!* We're in London."

The gleam in her eyes told him she was thinking that London was close to home. "And then?"

"I have some work to do at my London office. I need to meet with a few people about a chain of department stores I want to acquire in Europe." *Where they'll sell woolens by Elgiva MacRoth,* he added silently.

Douglas jiggled her and cheerfully ogled her bouncing breasts. "You can spend the day shopping. I'll have a chauffeur take you to the best boutiques in the city. You can buy anything you want."

"I don't want to spend your money, Douglas. It would make me feel like a kept woman."

"So? I was your kept man for almost two weeks. Can't I get even?"

"You're twisting the meaning of the word, you beastie."

He tried not to push too hard, but her refusal to be drawn into his life-style worried him. "You're depriving me of the pleasure of sending you shopping. At least go window-shopping, if your independent little heart refuses to let you spend a pittance of my enormous fortune."

"Hah! You'll tell the chauffeur to make notes about everything that interests me, and you'll send someone to buy it for me later."

He gave her an exasperated look. "You know me *too* well."

"No." She kissed him. "Not well enough. But I'm studying you."

Douglas regarded her somberly. *Patience, Kincaid, patience.* "Then you probably know that I'll fly you up to Scotland after my business is finished in London."

"Aye!" She smiled brightly. "I'll show you around. We'll go to MacRoth Hall, and you and my brother can make friends. Oh, Douglas, thank you, thank you. This has all turned out so well! I can't wait to go home!"

She snuggled her head on his shoulder and hugged him. He held her tightly, feeling jealous of a place and a heritage that might take her away from him if he weren't very careful.

Ten

"I've visited London before," she told him the next morning. "But never like this."

Douglas watched with serene, smiling love as she moved about the main room of their enormous hotel suite, her artistic fingers absorbing the gilt and brocade of old-world elegance. She was particularly happy today—she'd called her brother and convinced him to meet them in Scotland tomorrow. Douglas nodded to himself. He'd win Rob MacRoth's friendship as his next step in the permanent acquisition of Elgiva's affections.

But for now he didn't want to think about that. He simply wanted to enjoy looking at her. A floor-length dressing gown whispered around her ankles. The morning light filtered through the silk sheers covering a tall window and made a reddish-gold halo at the crown of her head.

She was her own best creation, her own work of art, and if he never wanted to share this view of her with anyone else, who could blame him? A connoisseur had a right to be selfish about a masterpiece.

Douglas fiddled with his gold cuff links and took extra time straightening his black vest. He slipped into the black jacket of an exquisitely tailored suit and sighed in dismay. He was already late for the

9:00 A.M. meeting at his London office building, head-quarters of British Kincaid. For the first time in years he wanted to skip work.

"The chauffeur will be waiting at ten," he reminded Elgiva. "I wish you'd go shopping."

She came to him and kissed his mouth firmly. "Off to work with you, dear man. I'm going to the museums."

"All right. But when you get to the Fordham, at least let the curator be your personal guide. It's all set up. Do that much for me. I mean, I ought to get *something* in return for all the money I donated to his place."

"You're a charitable man, Douglas," she said with a slightly taunting smile, both amused and rebuking.

He grunted. "Unsentimental."

"We'll see about that." She kissed him again, using her tongue in delicate, delicious ways, and by the time he left the suite, he was so distracted that he bumped into a waiter in the hallway and knocked him down.

Douglas helped the man rise, waved his humble apologies aside, and pressed a hundred-pound note into his astonished hand. Then he strode away, whistling the strains of a Scottish jig.

"You admire the legends connected with these gems more than the gems themselves," the dapper little curator at the Fordham told her.

Elgiva smiled. "Oh, I've got naught against fine jewelry, but the legends are safer to carry about." She nodded at the thick glass cases anchored in marble. "Wouldn't you say?"

The tweedy little man chuckled. "Indeed." They walked farther along the museum's display. "This is one of the world's finest collections of famous gems," the curator mentioned.

They arrived at a case that held a glittering necklace of teardrop-shaped diamonds. "They're incredible," Elgiva whispered in awe.

"They're the Tears of Simone. Commissioned by the father of a French baroness, as a consolation gift for forcing her to marry a man she disliked. There's a companion necklace called the Smiles of Simone. Her husband had it created to commemorate their tenth anniversary—a happy one, as it turned out. The Smiles of Simone are magnificent sapphires."

Elgiva looked up quickly. Sapphires. She struggled not to grimace. "Do you have the Smiles of Simone here?"

The curator looked puzzled. "Why, no. I thought you knew. Mr. Kincaid has been negotiating to purchase them from an Arabian collector, a patron of ours. I believe the sale was finalized last week."

Elgiva stared at him. A hollow, distraught feeling began to grow inside her chest, even as she told herself not to read too much into Douglas's deal. But her enjoyment of London and her bright hopes for the future had dimmed. So he was still adding to his collection.

He still wanted sapphires for a blond, blue-eyed wife. She touched a fingertip to the corner of one amber eye. Douglas had become color-blind, but not for long, it seemed.

She delayed returning to the hotel. She had the chauffeur take her to famous sites in the city, where she wandered about and pretended to be intrigued. But her thoughts were riveted painfully to the news that Douglas had purchased more sapphires.

She was no daydreaming child, she told herself; she was thirty-four, a widow, a self-supporting businesswoman, and a practical person who knew better than to weave bold threads when gossamer ones were expected. Douglas cared for her—there was no doubt of it. But he didn't necessarily love her. People didn't have to love each other to become lovers—even when to one of them the love was all consuming.

•　　•　　•

"Monsieur, Dr. MacCannon is here." Gert's voice was soft and dulcet toned, which meant that the doctor was standing nearby. Otherwise Gert would have made the announcement like a brusque little general.

Douglas set a stack of paperwork aside on a gleaming rosewood desk and punched a button on the phone console. "Refresh my memory, Gert."

"The Kincaid genealogy research. You have an appointment to discuss his findings. I hired him from the university of Scotland. He's an expert on Scottish history."

Excitement surged through Douglas's veins. "Send him in!"

A short, rotund man who resembled a Scottish Dr. Watson tromped into the darkly paneled office, stocky arms pumping exuberantly inside a plaid coat. Douglas stood and extended a hand. "Nice to meet you, Dr. MacCannon. I'm Douglas Kincaid."

Dr. MacCannon bounced Douglas's hand vigorously and grinned. Then he bellowed, " 'Tis nice to meet the thirty-fifth Duke of Talrigh, direct descendant of Gregory the Wolf, distant relative of half the ancient kings of Scotland, and by rights the chief of the Kincaid clan." He paused, frowning solemnly, then added, "Of which a cruel fate left none but the American branch."

Stunned, Douglas asked slowly, "Then it's true? The Kincaids were an important clan in Scotland? And they were all killed except one who went to America?"

"Aye."

Douglas gestured to an armchair. "Please, have a seat. And tell me everything." As the historian dropped into the chair, Douglas stared at him in continuing astonishment. Guilt assailed him as he recalled how he'd doubted Elgiva and fought her attempts to convince him of his Scottish background.

He could barely wait to apologize. He couldn't wait to tell her about the pride that he felt at the idea of sharing this wonderful bond with her. Douglas planted both hands on his desktop and leaned toward Dr. MacCannon, dozens of questions crowding his throat. He knew which one he had to ask first.

"Damned good work, doc! So tell me, who were the rats who rubbed out my clan?"

Dr. MacCannon blinked quizzically at the gangster lingo. Then understanding dawned. "Och! They rubbed them out, that's for sure! Rubbed them out and left only Tammas Kincaid alive—and him they put on a ship for America! They rubbed out the whole bunch and destroyed Castle Talrigh!"

Douglas leaned forward even more, his fascination mingling with dismay over all that some barbaric clan had stolen from his ancestors, and therefore from him. "Who?" he demanded. "Who murdered my relatives?"

The historian clasped his chest dramatically. *"The grrreat and powerrrful clan of MacRoth."*

The phone rang in the breakfast nook at 6:00 A.M. while Douglas was out jogging. Elgiva stared dully across her untouched porridge and willed the phone to be quiet. Douglas kept this hotel suite permanently, so he'd had phones installed everywhere, and it was disconcerting.

This particular phone squatted on the breakfast table where he'd left it after swallowing a cup of coffee and checking with Gert for messages. When it refused to be quiet, Elgiva picked the receiver up. "Good morning, Gert."

"Good morning, Madame MacRoth. Your brother is on the line."

Elgiva frowned in bewilderment. "Thank you."

"Ellie, are you where you can talk freely?" Rob's deep voice was low and furious.

"Aye. What's wrong?"

"Where's that bastard Kincaid?"

"He's gone to exercise." Elgiva clutched the phone

so tightly that her fingers ached. "Robbie, what's the matter?"

"He lied to you, Ellie. I've been keeping tabs on him. He charmed you with his so-called change of heart and used you without any remorse. Get yourself together and leave before he comes back, Ellie. I'll drive Duncan's truck down to London and pick you up—"

"Robbie! What are you accusing Douglas of doing?" Elgiva hunched forward, girding herself for an invisible blow.

Rob's soft, fierce voice sizzled in the phone. "He's bought the estate, Ellie. He bought it yesterday."

Gert and her staff of ten met Douglas when he reentered the hotel lobby. "Good morning, Monsieur K," Gert said, and handed him a towel.

"Good morning." He wiped his face briskly and tossed the towel over one shoulder of his black sweats.

His thoughts distracted by the day's plans with Elgiva, Douglas conducted a brusque business meeting as Gert and her staff followed him toward his private elevator. He felt like a battleship being followed by puffing little tugs.

He finished the meeting by the time he and the group reached the hotel's penthouse. "One more thing," Gert told him as he stepped into the hall. "Madame MacRoth asked me to change the itinerary for today's trip to Scotland. I've made the new arrangements."

Douglas halted and frowned at her in surprise. "What did she ask you to do?"

"She requests that your pilot fly into the mountains rather than to her village. To the cottage there." Gert cut her eyes in private communication with him. *Your former jail,* she indicated, amusement in her eyes. "She also asked me to have the hotel fix a hamper of food for an overnight stay. I've done so."

"All right. Thank you. We'll be back late tomorrow afternoon."

"*Bon soir*, Monsieur."

As Douglas strode down the hall he jerked the towel into his hands and twisted it fiercely. Now that he knew the history of the MacRoths and the Kincaids, he understood why Elgiva might not want to love him. What was her plan, to take him back to the scene of their early feud so that he'd remember all their differences? To tell him that a MacRoth would never stoop to love a Kincaid?

He stopped outside the doors to the suite and took several calming breaths. Patience. Compromise. History was *not* going to repeat itself. This time the Kincaids would be the victors.

Elgiva thought that her nerves would snap if she didn't get the truth from Douglas soon.

Sitting next to one of the helicopter's large, tinted windows, she stroked Sam's golden head and stared resolutely at the rugged land dotted with small farms and flocks of sheep. The ruins of a medieval castle rose jaggedly from a hill overlooking a village.

"We'll visit an even grander place," she promised Sam. "I'm taking you and Douglas on a hike to Castle Talrigh today."

Elgiva shut her eyes and heard Rob's sinister words: "Aye, draw the bastard there, Ellie. We'll be waiting."

But before anyone else confronted Douglas, she had to hear for herself that he'd betrayed her; she was dying inside, but she had to give him a chance to explain.

Exhausted from the strain of pretending to be cheerful, Elgiva glanced over at Douglas and was grateful to find him asleep. He was stretched out in a plush reclining seat next to the opposite window, stereo headphones covering his ears.

She ached with new despair—now that he was dressed in corduroys, hiking boots, a sweater, and a heavy outdoorsman's jacket, he seemed more like her own people and less like a raider from a different world. How deceptive could he be? Elgiva glanced down at herself. She wore similar hiking clothes, with a plump, quilted jacket covered in shiny silver material.

It was a gift from the man who had probably lied to her. The one thing about which he had not lied, it seemed, was their relationship. He'd never said that he loved her or talked about sharing a future with her.

She turned blindly to the window. Sam rested his muzzle on her knee and peered out, his ears at half-mast as he studied the scenery below.

Elgiva gripped his ruff and whispered, " 'Tis the land of Shakespeare's evil Macbeth, lad. But in truth, Macbeth was not a bad king. He ruled for many years, and his vassals thought well of him." She rested her cheek against Sam's head. "I wish that the truth were always so much kinder than the legend."

Elgiva couldn't tell from his silence if Douglas were awed or bored. She was so filled with apprehension that she didn't feel like talking, either.

They stood on the edge of the deep, purple-black waters of Loch Talrigh and looked at the ghostly ruins of the castle, growing from its rocky island like a natural formation. The loch curled around the island less than a man's height from the castle's foundation.

A light fog rose from the water, and a capricious afternoon sun occasionally moved from behind gray clouds to light the fog from behind. When it did, the castle was shrouded in a silver mist.

It was grand even in ruins. Majestic turrets jutted upward from the corners of crumbling battlements; squares of light showed where windows had once adorned the upper chambers. Elgiva looked at Douglas and said as casually as she could, "It was built in the thirteenth century."

He nodded. "Castle Talrigh." He turned dark, unreadable eyes to her. "You tried to tell me once that this was the castle of the Kincaids."

"I didn't bring you here to lecture you about history that you don't want to know," she said without rebuke. "Just come and see the place."

He nodded again, his eyes never ceasing to study her. "Should I spread my old cynicism on the water like Sir Walter Raleigh's cloak, so that we can walk?"

"No. You can put your cynicism on the seat of a rowboat."

Elgiva glanced at the faint outline of the old stone causeway, a few feet away. She had her reasons for not telling him about it. She checked her wristwatch. The others would be here soon.

"Come along," she said, and gestured for him to follow. In a clump of trees she found the creaky rowboat a fisherman had left long ago and never reclaimed.

"I'm glad I taught you to swim," Douglas muttered, when they were halfway across the dark, still loch. He pulled the oars with careful movements, as if fearing that the boat would fall apart at any moment. "Sam, if you sneeze, I'll never forgive you."

Snuffling, Sam hunched closer to Elgiva's legs and looked around nervously.

Soon the castle loomed over them, casting a cold shadow. They left the boat on the rock-strewn shore, and Elgiva led the way up a steep walk to a ragged archway set in the stone. "Welcome to the past," she said softly. Her pulse raced, and a sense of dread filled her.

Wind whistled through the narrow chamber that took them to the castle's interior. "Here's the heart of the place," Elgiva announced, sweeping her arms about her. "It was once the great hall. Imagine it with a tall, arching roof of heavy timbers and tapestries covering the walls."

She pointed to the cavernous fireplaces on either side. "With cheerful blazes there and the castle lord's dogs curled up on the hearth rugs." Elgiva gestured to mysterious stone supports that poked out from an upper section of one wall. "There was a gallery for the minstrels. You can almost hear their music if you listen with your imagination."

"You love this place," Douglas commented.

"Well, I feel a wee bit possessive about it. It's so far from the tourist track that few people ever come to see it. It's a special place for those of us who appreciate the history."

"Even when it's not MacRoth history?"

Clutching her hands in front of her, she eyed him with growing distress. It was time to talk. "Well, we MacRoths lost our castle, you see. It was destroyed by the English. It was at the site of the current hall."

"So you've adopted this castle instead?"

"Aye." She shoved her hands into her jacket pockets. "Come along." She led him into a courtyard closely surrounded by stone walls. The stark openings of doors and windows looked down on them from all sides, like sightless eyes. Elgiva was unnerved by the way Douglas went to the center of the courtyard and stood there, tall and silent, his head turning majestically as he studied the place.

His gaze dropped to her. His eyes flashed with pride and satisfaction—an almost fierce light of possession that seemed to encompass her as well. "El," he said slowly, "I know everything that happened between the MacRoths and the Kincaids. I apologize for doubting your stories. I hired someone to research what you'd told me. I know the entire history, right up to the battle that destroyed this castle."

Elgiva swayed in place and stared at him with horrified understanding. "Then you're wanting revenge," she said in a low, furious voice. "I see. That's why you lied to me."

He quickly moved toward her. "Lied to you? How?"

"You bought the MacRoth estate yesterday!"

He halted. For several seconds he was silent, scowling. "Yes," he said finally. "It was supposed to be a surprise. How the hell did you find out?"

"A *surprise*?" She began to tremble with fury and heartache. "You coldhearted thief! My brother never trusted you, and he kept a watch on you through some friends of his in the government! He called me this morning and told me what you'd done!"

"Remind me to throttle his bagpipes."

A gunshot ran out in the distance. Elgiva turned and ran to a narrow stone staircase that climbed one wall. "Explain your treachery to my clan," she called to Douglas. "They'll make the last fight between the MacRoths and the Kincaids look like a picnic."

Her heart caught in her throat when she heard Douglas following her. Sam danced back and forth in the courtyard and barked. Elgiva climbed all the way to the battlements and stepped onto their stone catwalk. Douglas appeared a second later. She clasped the outer wall for balance and backed away from him. His expression was fierce as he advanced on her.

"I don't care if our clans spent seven centuries trying to kill each other," he said raspily, his voice black with anger. "I don't care if what's left of your clan wants to finish what their ancestors started. But *you*"—he jabbed a hand at her and kept advancing—"I thought you trusted me."

Elgiva reached a spot where the wall had crumpled inward, blocking her way. "I did! And you paid me back by taking what you'd promised to leave alone!"

A second gunshot exploded nearby, and the bullet smacked the outer wall somewhere below them. Douglas gripped the top of the wall and looked out over the loch. His mouth dropped open in amazement.

Two dozen angry people were walking across the water. Elgiva waved to Rob, who led the route along the zigzagging causeway. Duncan followed with his mother riding astride his back; then came Andrew, Dr. Graham, John Callum, Richard Maxwell, and others, including three aging servants from MacRoth Hall who'd always remained loyal to her and Rob.

"They've come to confront you, Douglas, and you can't bargain your way out of the trouble. So you'd better tell the truth about your plans for the village and the farms, as well as MacRoth Hall."

"If they want a battle, they've got it. But you're going to be on my side, this time." He snatched her by one wrist and pulled her back down the stairs. Tugging her behind him, he went to the center of the courtyard and stood defiantly. When she tried to leave, he wound an arm around her waist and held her still.

"Sam, go," he commanded, pointing to a distant corner. Sam reluctantly obeyed. "Stay."

"They won't hurt an innocent dog," Elgiva said angrily.

"Oh?" His eyes flashed a challenge. "The MacRoths kept this castle under seige when they knew that women and children were starving here."

"Because the Kincaid men were too proud to admit defeat!"

"And the MacRoths didn't have that problem, huh? You stole a jeweled brooch from the wife of the Kincaid chieftain, and then refused to give it back."

"Aye, but that was just a petty bit of fun by some of the young men in the clan. We were negotiating to return the bauble when you Kincaids tricked half of our men into a meeting—offered them hospitality, your clan did—and then murdered them treacherously!"

"We didn't deserve to be banished by the Crown for one mistake! The MacRoths and Kincaids had been killing each other for centuries!"

"You broke the bond of honor when you lured your enemies into such a trap! The sharing of hearth and home was always a sacred covenant of truce!"

"We didn't break the rules, we only bent them!"

"Och! Spoken like a true Kincaid!"

"Don't you have any compassion for the women and children who died here?"

"Aye, but they wouldn't have died if they'd surrendered! The MacRoths offered them the chance, Douglas, but they wouldn't take it!"

"Maybe they preferred to die on Scottish soil rather than be shipped to the colonies like criminals!"

"You better be glad that Tammas Kincaid was captured and sent off to start a new life, or you'd be naught but a twinkle in a ghost's eye right now!"

"Yes, my family survived, thank God. *The Kincaids*," he intoned drolly. "We're bad. We're back. And now, as lord of this castle, I'm not going to put up with any trouble from any MacRoths."

With fine timing Rob strode into the courtyard, his rubber boots slinging drops of water, a long overcoat whipping back from his big, powerful body, his brawny hands already clenched into fists. The others crowded in after him.

"Welcome, MacRoths," Douglas said loudly.

Rob stopped an arm's length away, his chest heaving with anger. "Let go of my sister and put up your fists, Kincaid."

"I'll do one—temporarily—but not the other."

Douglas released her and, putting a hand on her shoulder, gently pushed her aside. He looked straight into Rob's eyes and said calmly, "I won't fight with you."

Rob grunted with disdain. "You're a Kincaid. You like nothing better than to prove yourself. You'll fight."

Douglas let both hands hang loosely by his sides. "No."

Rob's fist flashed out with lethal surprise and smashed into Douglas's mouth. Douglas staggered but made no move to retaliate. A thick stream of blood slipped from a gash on his lower lip.

"Stop this!" Elgiva ordered frantically.

"Fight, Kincaid," Rob growled.

Douglas shot him a patronizing smile. "Kiss my tam-o'-shanter."

Rob punched him again. Douglas nearly fell down. Regaining his balance, he wavered drunkenly but refused to raise a hand in self-defense.

Elgiva leapt forward. "Why? Why are you doing this?" she begged, grasping Douglas's jacket. "Why won't you fight back?"

His mouth bleeding profusely now, his eyes squinting with pain, he looked down at her and said softly, "Because one of us has to compromise if this feud's ever going to end." He paused, his gaze searing her with its intensity. "Because he's your brother, and I don't want to hurt him. Because I love you."

Elgiva's knees went weak. She studied Douglas's eyes until she couldn't see through the blur of her own tears. Dimly she was aware of everyone gathering around them to watch and listen. "If you love me, why did you buy the estate?"

" 'War and wizardry—neither shall save them,' " he quoted. " 'Only true love shall soothe the pain and heal wounds of the past, that ancient sorrows may sleep at last.' " He smiled wearily. "I'm an actor at heart—I have a good memory for lines. The researcher I hired showed me that poem, and I read it at least a dozen times."

"But I still don't—"

"Knowing how seriously you take your family history, I was afraid that you'd never forgive and forget. I decided that one of my grand gestures was needed."

"He's trying to talk his way out of trouble, Ellie," Rob interjected.

Douglas never took his gaze from hers. "No, El. My gesture backfired, that's all."

With a shaking hand she reached up and wiped blood from his chin. "What did you think I'd do when you told me you'd bought my home?"

He grasped her arms and pulled her closer. "I thought you'd marry me."

Mutters and yelps came from the crowd around

them. "Strange way of thinking these Americans have," Duncan said, sneering.

"I think he's addled from Robbie's beating," Andrew observed.

"Hit him again," Mrs. M ordered.

Elgiva's grip tightened on Douglas's jacket. He looked a bit disheveled from Rob's powerful blows—blows that would have knocked most men flat—but he didn't seem confused. *Marry him?*

"I know we'd have to agree on some changes in our lives," he told her. "But we can do that. Do you ever think about marrying me?" he asked. "Even though I'm a Kincaid?"

Elgiva gazed at him blankly. "I think about it all the time."

A large, incredulous smile slid across his mouth despite the painful-looking injury. "My Lord, El, I didn't know. I thought—"

"Why would I have told you? You said that I'm not blond, I'm not blue-eyed, I'm not—"

"Very good at remembering details," he finished. "Otherwise you'd recall that I said all that during a time when you had accused me of a lot of disgusting things, called me names, rapped my knuckles with a piece of firewood, tried to feed me into a stupor, and pretended to fall asleep when I did a striptease. I would have said *anything* to aggravate you in return."

"But . . . the sapphires, for a blue-eyed blonde. Douglas, I know that you just bought another piece to add to your collection." She told him what the museum curator had said.

He chuckled. "I do collect sapphires. But you should see my collection of emeralds. Yes." He touched her chestnut hair, and his eyes gleamed with plans. "Yes," he said, his voice softer, "you'll like wearing the sapphires, but you'll love wearing the emeralds."

"Ellie, he's bluffing," Rob warned, but he sounded perplexed.

Elgiva shook her head numbly. "Douglas, why did you think that buying the MacRoth inheritance out from under me and my brother would make me want to marry you?"

"Because I was going to present it to you as an engagement gift." He winced. "Because I *am* presenting it to you as an engagement gift."

"You mean that if I don't marry you, you'll keep the estate?"

"Now the plan shows its true colors," Rob said darkly.

Elgiva looked into Douglas's gently rebuking eyes for a long time. "That's not what he meant at all, Rob," she whispered. "He would have given the estate back whether I said yes to the marriage or not."

"Sure," Duncan said sarcastically. "He paid for something you would have owned anyway, so he could give it to you. He donated a lot of money to old Angus's estate for nothing, because it's all been willed to the Bank of Scotland. Douglas Kincaid gave a donation to the Bank of Scotland just to make a sentimental gesture! Hoots, man! That's a fairy tale!"

Douglas never stopped looking into her eyes. He seemed lost to the world around them, and she was beginning to feel the same way. "I trust him," she announced. Then, much softer and to him alone, "I think you've come to appreciate fairy tales a bit." Elgiva rose on tiptoe and kissed the unhurt corner of his mouth.

He took her in his arms and held her tightly, his mouth against her ear, moving privately and whispering so that only she could hear, "I love you. I love you, you beautiful MacRoth."

"Everybody make friends with Mr. Kincaid," Mrs. M commanded in her most authoritative classroom voice. "If he backs out on his marriage proposal, *then* we'll give him a beating."

Elgiva leaned away from Douglas and looked at him with despair. "Now wait, wait—"

"Do you love me?" he asked, frowning at her reluctance.

"Oh, dear man, can't you see it? Can't you see that I love you so much that it makes me miserable?"

"That's not quite the way I wanted you to say it, El."

She took his face between her hands. "Douglas, have you forgotten? I may not be able to have children. How would you feel if I couldn't?"

"Disappointed." He kissed her. "But not sorry that I married you. I helped raise Kash Santelli—I know how I feel about being an adoptive parent. I'd be happy with that. After all, wasn't it common for us Scots to take the name of our clan's chief? Adopting kids would be a fine way to make certain that there are plenty of Kincaids in the world to keep the MacRoths under control."

He smiled wickedly. "Blood relatives or not, you're all frighteningly alike in temperament." Douglas's smile faded and he looked at Elgiva seriously. "Marry me. I love you. I'll be good to you and good to everyone and everything that you love." He paused and glanced over her shoulder at Rob. "Even him."

Elgiva twisted to look at her brother. Rob glared from Douglas to her. "If he marries you, I'll accept him," Rob told her. "But he's still a Kincaid, Ellie. Are you sure you want to take his name?"

Elgiva turned back to the man who held her with such possessive arms. "I'll always be a MacRoth," she murmured, losing herself in eyes as handsome as those of a Terkleshire wolf, but not wild at all, at least for the moment. They were frowning at her pride a wee bit, but loving her for it, and promising to share their secret delights with her for the rest of her life.

"I'll always be a MacRoth," she repeated, making her tone a little smug, "but I won't mind bearing the Kincaid name too."

Douglas kissed her. Then he lifted his head to the surrounding crowd, but looked above them as if he might also be addressing the castle and the spirits of all the Kincaids who had lived, and died, there. "I,

Douglas Kincaid, the Duke of Talrigh, chief of the clan of Kincaid, declare permanent peace between the Kincaids and the MacRoths. Let love soothe what war and wizardry—and kidnapping—could not."

He lowered his gaze to Elgiva. "Now, Elgiva MacRoth, will you seal this peace treaty by marrying me?"

Elgiva put her arms around his neck and told him, smiling, that she would.

They stood in the moonlight by a lovely old window, wrapped inside a blanket and each other's arms. She shivered a little from the drafts that crept across their bare feet, and Douglas pulled her closer. His contentment made him chuckle softly. He had a split lip, he'd spent a bundle on an estate that he hadn't needed to buy, and then he'd given it away. Now he was spending the night in one of the expensive bedrooms that he'd bought and given away, a cold bedroom full of ugly Victorian furniture and ancient dust motes.

But he'd never been happier in his whole life.

Elgiva tilted her head and brushed a careful kiss across his injured mouth. Her hands slid up and down his back, stroking affectionately. She rubbed her naked chest against his naked chest and gave him a look of naughty invitation from under one arched brow.

He smiled. He winced with pain. He smiled. He chuckled at his good luck.

"Douglas Kincaid, I think you're delightfully off-center tonight," she told him.

"I love you so much."

Happiness glimmered in her eyes. "Dear man, stay off-center. I'll do my best to keep you there." She took his hands and began to draw him toward a rumpled, four-poster bed. "You poor, injured darling. Come let true love soothe your pain a bit more."

"True love. Are we talking about legends again?"

She pulled him down on the bed, where they were

soon intimately bundled under the covers. "Aye, and promises for future legends," she assured him.

Douglas felt the sweet, giving touch of her hands and saw the devotion in her eyes. "I believe you," he whispered.

"Believe this—I'm going to spend the rest of my life showing you that a MacRoth knows how to make a Kincaid deliriously happy."

"But no better than a Kincaid knows how to keep a MacRoth happy."

"Is that a challenge, you *arrogant* Kincaid?"

"You betcha, MacRoth."

And he kissed her, just to get some trouble started.

THE EDITOR'S CORNER

May is a special month here at LOVESWEPT. It's our anniversary month! We began publishing LOVESWEPTs in May 1983, and with your encouragement and support we've been at it ever since. One of the hallmarks of the LOVESWEPT line has always been our focus on our authors. The six authors whose books you can look forward to next month represent what we feel is the true strength of our line—a blend of your favorite tried-and-true authors along with several talented newcomers. The books these wonderful writers have penned just for you are as unique and different as the ladies themselves.

Helen Mittermeyer leads off the month with the second book in her *Men of Ice* trilogy, **BLACK FROST,** LOVESWEPT #396. Helen's legions of fans often remark on the intensity of emotion between her characters and the heightened sense of drama in her novels. She won't disappoint you at all with **BLACK FROST!** Hero Bear Kenmore, a race-car driver with nerves of steel, gets the thrill of his life when he meets heroine Kip Noble. Bear has never met a woman whose courage and daring equals his own, but Kip is his match in every way. For Kip, falling in love with Bear is like jumping into an inferno. She's irrevocably drawn to him yet has to struggle to keep her independence. Helen has once again created characters who barely keep from spontaneously combusting when they're together. Helen's "men of ice" are anything but!

Jan Hudson's latest treat is **STEP INTO MY PARLOR,** LOVESWEPT #397. With three previous books to her credit, this sassy Texas lady has captured your attention and doesn't plan to let it go! She brings characters to life who are true to themselves in every way and as straightforward as Jan herself. You'll enjoy the ride as her unabashedly virile hero, Spider Webb, falls hard for lovely socialite Anne Foxworth Jennings. Anne is out of cash and nearly out of hope when she meets the seductive pirate, Spider. He almost makes her forget she has to stay one step ahead of the man who'd threatened her life. But in Spider's arms she's spellbound, left breathless with yearning. Caught in his tender web, Anne discovers that she no longer fears for her life because Spider has captured her soul. **STEP INTO MY PARLOR** will grab you from page one!

Joan Elliott Pickart's **WHISPERED WISHES,** LOVESWEPT

(continued)

#398, tells the love story of Amnity Ames and Tander Ellis. You may remember Tander as the sexy computer expert friend of the hero from **MIXED SIGNALS,** #386. Joan just had to give Tander his due, and he falls for Amnity like a rock! Can you imagine a gorgeous hunk walking into a crafts store and telling the saleswoman he's decided to take up needlepoint! Tander does just that and Amnity never suspects he's got ulterior motives—she's too busy trying to catch her breath. Joan's characters always testify to the fact that there is a magical thing called love at first sight. Her books help renew your spirit and gladden your heart. You won't be able to resist feeling an emotional tug when Amnity whispers her wishes to Tander. Enjoy this special story!

One of the newcomers to LOVESWEPT is Terry Lawrence— an author we think has an exciting future ahead of her. You may have read Terry's first LOVESWEPT, **WHERE THERE'S SMOKE, THERE'S FIRE,** which was published in the fall of 1988. Since then, Terry has been hard at work and next month her second book for us hits the shelves, **THE OUTSIDER,** LOVESWEPT #399. Both the hero and the heroine of this sensually charged romance know what it's like to be outsiders, and in each other's arms they discover what it feels like to belong. When Joe Bond catches Susannah Moran switching dice in the casino he manages in his Ottawa Indian community, he has to admit the lady is good— and temptingly beautiful. Just doing her job investigating the casino's practices, Susannah has to admit she's never been caught so fast and never by a man who set off alarms all over her body! These two special people don't find it easy to bridge the differences between their cultures. But what does come easily is the overwhelming need and desire they feel for each other. Terry will surely win loads of new readers with this tender, evocatively written love story. You'll want to count yourself among them!

We published Patt Bucheister's very first LOVESWEPT, **NIGHT AND DAY,** back in early 1986, and what a smash debut it was! Now, many books and many fans later, Patt presents you with another delicious delight, **THE ROGUE,** LOVESWEPT #400. A warm and generous lady with a sunny disposition, Patt naturally creates such a heroine in Meredith Claryon. When Meredith receives a strange phone call one night from a man demanding she answer his ques-

(continued)

tions, Meredith handles the situation with her usual grace and aplomb. Paul Rouchett is so intrigued by the lady he's never met that he decides he has no choice but to convince her to team up with him to find the embezzler who'd robbed his nightclub and run off with her sister. And what a team they make! The tart-tongued nurse and the owner of the Rogue's Den are an unbeatable duo—but discovering that for themselves leads them on a merry, romantic chase. Patt's strong belief in love and romance couldn't come across better than in this well-crafted book.

Have you every wondered exactly what makes a guy a good ol' boy? Having lived my entire life north of the Mason-Dixon line, I can tell you I have! But after reading **LOVIN' A GOOD OL' BOY** by Mary Kay McComas, LOVESWEPT #401, I wonder no more. Hero Buck LaSalle is a good ol' boy in the flesh, and when Yankee Anne Hunnicut hits town in her high heels and designer suits, Buck leaves no doubt in her mind about the term. He has the sexiest smile she's ever seen and too much charm for his own good, and although he's none too pleased about why she's there, he shows her in more ways than she ever imagined how much he wants her to stay. With her inimitable style, Mary Kay will have you giggling or sighing with pleasure or shedding a tear—probably all three—before you finish this sure-to-please romance. You'll long for a good ol' boy of your own.

Since we like to set the books in our anniversary month apart, we're going to surprise you with our cover design next month. But you're used to surprises from us, right? It makes life more interesting—and fun!

All best wishes.

Sincerely,

Susann Brailey

Susann Brailey
Editor
LOVESWEPT
Bantam Books
666 Fifth Avenue
New York, NY 10103

FAN OF THE MONTH

Jane Calleja

It was the colorful cover which prompted me to buy my first LOVESWEPT. I was already an avid reader of romance books then, but the unique stories and interesting characters in the LOVESWEPTs brought new meaning to romance for me.

New issues arrived here in the Philippines each month featuring original and delightful plots. I fell in love with the heroes and heroines of Barbara Boswell, Iris Johansen, Fayrene Preston, Joan Elliott Pickart, Kay Hooper, and Sandra Brown. The authors were able to capture everyday human emotions and make their characters come alive. I would like to thank these writers for answering my letters despite their hectic schedules.

My wish is to be able to join the ranks of the LOVESWEPT authors in the future. Right now I am nineteen years old and a third-year college student. I love reading LOVESWEPTs so much that I read the same books over and over again. In fact, I've read **FOR THE LOVE OF SAMI** by Fayrene Preston more than ten times, and I plan to read it again soon. Once I start to read, I really lose track of time and place. My family just watches me queerly if I suddenly giggle or cry in the middle of reading a book. That's how vivid LOVESWEPTs are! You can't help but feel what the characters are feeling.

I was surprised, but honored and delighted to be chosen a Fan of the Month. Thank you!

THE DELANEY DYNASTY

THE SHAMROCK TRINITY

- ☐ 21975 RAFE, THE MAVERICK
  by Kay Hooper $2.95
- ☐ 21976 YORK, THE RENEGADE
  by Iris Johansen $2.95
- ☐ 21977 BURKE, THE KINGPIN
  by Fayrene Preston $2.95

THE DELANEYS OF KILLAROO

- ☐ 21872 ADELAIDE, THE ENCHANTRESS
  by Kay Hooper $2.75
- ☐ 21873 MATILDA, THE ADVENTURESS
  by Iris Johansen $2.75
- ☐ 21874 SYDNEY, THE TEMPTRESS
  by Fayrene Preston $2.75

THE DELANEYS: *The Untamed Years*

- ☐ 21899 GOLDEN FLAMES *by Kay Hooper* $3.50
- ☐ 21898 WILD SILVER *by Iris Johansen* $3.50
- ☐ 21897 COPPER FIRE *by Fayrene Preston* $3.50

THE DELANEYS II

- ☐ 21978 SATIN ICE *by Iris Johansen* $3.50
- ☐ 21979 SILKEN THUNDER *by Fayrene Preston* $3.50
- ☐ 21980 VELVET LIGHTNING *by Kay Hooper* $3.50

Bantam Books, Dept. SW7, 414 East Golf Road, Des Plaines, IL 60016

Please send me the items I have checked above. I am enclosing $_____
(please add $2.00 to cover postage and handling). Send check or money
order, no cash or C.O.D.s please.

Mr/Ms _____

Address _____

City/State_____ Zip_____

SW7–4/90

Please allow four to six weeks for delivery.
Prices and availability subject to change without notice.

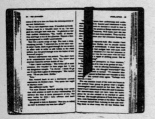